MW01634058

SEARCHING FOR HAVEN (SPECIAL FORCES: OPERATION ALPHA)

FALLPORT RESCUE OPERATIONS
BOOK TWO

JEN TALTY

Dear Readers,

Welcome to the Special Forces: Operation Alpha Fan-Fiction world!

If you are new to this amazing world, in a nutshell the author wrote a story using one or more of my characters in it. Sometimes that character has a major role in the story, and other times they are only mentioned briefly. This is perfectly legal and allowable because they are going through Aces Press to publish the story.

This book is entirely the work of the author who wrote it. While I might have assisted with brainstorming and other ideas about which of my characters to use, I didn't have any part in the process or writing or editing the story.

I'm proud and excited that so many authors loved my characters enough that they wanted to write them into their own story. Thank you for supporting them, and me!

READ ON!
Xoxo
Susan Stoker

CHAPTER ONE

Weston Campbell fiddled with the label on his beer. He sat in a booth in the back of On the Rocks bar. He'd prepared a speech. He'd practiced it a hundred times on his drive, but the words didn't come.

His cousins, Rocky and Ethan Watson, glared with their own special brand of judgment. There was a part of Weston that didn't blame them. His life had been riddled with failure. He could try to explain what happened, but what would be the point? Rocky and Ethan—like most people—only focused on the result.

Dishonorable discharge.

The shame that Weston had brought to the family and to himself was a cross he'd been bearing his entire life. At thirty-five, he had nothing but a string of bad decisions, unfortunate mistakes, and one major incident that honestly hadn't been his fault, but at the end of the day, that mission had been his responsibility. The success—or failure—had lain solely on his shoulders.

"We're giving you a chance because you're family," Rocky said, finally breaking the horrifying silence. "But outside of that, there will be no special treatment. You will pull your weight and do as you're told."

Growing up, he and his cousins had always been at odds. They were older and thought they knew better, which drove Weston fucking nuts. Of course, he'd been a cocky son of a bitch, which didn't help. He could see how his behavior in the past only made him look like an asshole. He had a giant chip on his shoulder and set out to prove—hell, he had no idea what—but the Army knocked that chip right off pretty damn quick. However, his cousins hadn't been around to see that. They'd been so fed up with his shit they didn't bother to pay attention.

No one did.

Not even Weston's parents. When he'd been discharged, his folks hadn't been surprised and told him he'd ruined the only good thing that had ever happened to him.

No shit.

"I don't expect any special treatment, but it would be nice to be seen as the adult that I am and not the small child you remember." He held up his hand. "I don't need anyone to remind me of past mistakes, and I'm not going to sit here and play the blame game or feel sorry for myself. I can't change what happened. I can only move forward. You have my word that I will be a professional, both here at the bar and with the search and rescue team."

Ethan and Rocky exchanged glances, and not a way positive either. It was the same condescending arched brow they'd given him the last time they'd been together.

"That remains to be seen," Rocky said. "Actions speak louder than words."

Weston wanted to remind his cousins that it had been ten years since they'd been in the same room, much less spent any real time together, but he figured it was best to keep his big fat trap shut. Sarcasm had not been his friend as of late. Or ever.

"Are you settled into your apartment?" Ethan asked.

"I dropped my things off, but I haven't had the chance to unpack." Weston polished off his beer in two quick gulps. It went down hard and soured his already upset stomach. "I appreciate you helping me find an affordable place." It wasn't much. A small studio that came furnished with a couch, one chair, a television, a small table that fit two people, and a fully stocked kitchen. The bed was small, only a full size, but the mattress appeared comfortable. It had a privacy curtain separating the sleeping quarters and the living area, which was nice. He didn't need anything more. It was better than some of the other places he'd called home over the last ten years.

"This is a nice small town," Rocky said. "The people are welcoming."

"When can I start with search and rescue?" The idea he could put to use some of his skills he'd learned in the Army made the circumstances of his discharge sting a little less.

"You'll need to go through the training like everyone else and that starts this week. But if we have a situation, you'll be called." Rocky tapped his knuckles on the table. "Show us we can trust you."

"I will." Weston nodded.

"Here comes Zeke. He's doing us a favor by giving you a job when you're not working search and rescue. He's an ex-Green Beret and a good man. Don't fuck this up." Ethan slipped from the booth.

Rocky followed.

Weston stood. "I won't let you down." He stretched out his arm, shaking both of his cousins' hands.

"We'll see you tomorrow." Rocky nodded before strolling toward the front of the bar.

Weston stared at the backside of his cousins and wiggled his fingers. Guilt and shame filled his soul. The young boy inside wanted to tell them to fuck off, but the man knew this was his last chance. He had to prove he had what it took to make things right here and maybe he could do the same everywhere else.

"You must be the infamous Weston Campbell." Zeke slapped him on the back. "I've heard a lot about you."

"I'm sure most of it hasn't been stellar."

Zeke chuckled. "Well, it hasn't been great, but we all have a past and I believe in second chances, so you came to the right bar." He smiled. "Unfortunately for you, right now the only position I have open is bussing tables."

"I need to keep my mind and hands occupied, so it works for me," Weston said. "But if you ever need anything else, I've waited tables and know my way behind a bar. I'm happy to fill in anywhere."

"That's good to know." Zeke nodded.

"When can I start?"

"How about right now? I'm shorthanded and could use someone washing dishes."

"Sounds good. Point me in the right direction."

Zeke glanced over his shoulder. "Hey, Haven." He waved to a young woman who had delivered a tray of drinks to a group of five ladies. "Mind showing our newest employee to the kitchen? He's going to be doing the dishes for us tonight."

"Sure thing." Haven tucked her tray under her arm and scurried across the room.

The closer she got, the faster Weston's heart beat. Her long brown hair had been weaved into a braid. She wore very little makeup and her blue eyes sparkled in the dim lighting. Her jeans hugged her body like a wet suit and her white T-shirt hung loosely against her chest. He'd seen his share of beautiful women but never anyone as natural or as striking as Haven. Something about the way her smile lit up the room touched his aching heart.

"Welcome to On the Rocks," she said. "I saw you sitting with Rocky and Ethan. How do you know them?"

"They're my cousins," Weston admitted.

Her big blue orbs widened with the kind of

recognition that made Weston want to walk right on out of the bar.

Of course his cousin had told the entire town of his arrival and of his past. They probably even told her about Darlene.

What a fucking nightmare. Very few people knew the truth of what happened there and he stopped trying to correct his family a long time ago. They wanted to believe the worst. Based on who he'd been up until he turned twenty-two, he couldn't blame anyone for that, but he had changed. Darlene had been the one who broke his heart. But all his family saw was the spectacle he'd made of himself.

And the big fat lie Darlene had told the world.

"I heard you were coming," Haven said. "Why don't you follow me."

"Zeke, thanks for the opportunity. I really appreciate it."

"You're welcome," Zeke said. "I'll put you on the schedule and text it to you tomorrow."

Weston held his head high as he meandered into kitchen. It felt like every eye in the bar had been on him. As if everyone in the damn town had already heard his life story. He swallowed his pride and did his best to push down all the self-pity and hatred that tended to bubble through his veins. If he allowed it to surface, he didn't stand a chance in hell of turning his life around.

"When did you get into town?" Haven asked.

"Three hours ago."

"I can tell your ex-military. Were you a SEAL too?"

"Nope. I was in the Army. Ranger."

"Thank you for your service." She handed him an apron. "You're going to want to wear this. Otherwise, you will be soaking wet by the end of the night." She pointed to a big machine spitting water and steam. "That's a sterilizer. These racks you fill with beer mugs, water glasses, plates, anything but wineglasses and pots and pans." She pointed to an industrial-size sink. "Those you hand-wash in that. Make sure you dry the wineglasses right away and that they don't have any spots on them. Or that they smell funny."

"I can handle that."

"Good," she said. "Once the racks come out of the sterilizer, make sure everything is dry, and you can stack dishes over there, but glasses and stuff need to come back out to the bar area. Got it?"

"Seems simple enough."

"You have no idea how many people screw it up."

She leaned against the counter on the other side of the sink. "Mind if I ask you a personal question?"

"I might not answer, but sure, go ahead."

"Why are you working as a dishwasher?"

He laughed. "It's punishment for being an asshole."

"At least you're honest."

He arched a brow. "And what is that supposed to mean?"

"I was told to watch out for you, but I wasn't given too many details."

"My cousins and I haven't seen each other in years. They are basing that on old information and maybe a tainted viewpoint because of my discharge from the Army." Fuck. Loose lips sunk ships.

"They didn't say anything about that, but Zeke also told me to keep a safe distance. However, he's like a big overprotective brother. Kind of a pain, until it's not. He means well, and I really appreciate all he's done for me, but he can be overbearing at times."

"I know the feeling."

Zeke pushed open the door carrying a couple trays of dirty dishes. "Both of you need to get to work."

"I was just finishing up giving Weston the rundown." She curled her fingers around his biceps.

A hint of electricity shot through his system. He wasn't used to having members of the opposite sex affect him in such a primal way.

He suspected she was a good eight to ten years younger than he, and that was just too young. Besides, he wasn't here to meet women. That was the last thing he needed on his plate.

"Holler if you need anything." Haven disappeared into the bar.

Zeke stared Weston down. "I might be all about second chances, but she's off-limits. Do I make myself clear?"

Was this fucking grade school? "I'm here to work, nothing else."

"Look, let's not pretend I don't know your history."

Here we goddamned go. The tainted version one. The version full of half-truths seen through the lens of those who weren't there and didn't care to ask what really happened between him and Darlene. It was hard for Weston not to feel sorry for himself when this kept happening. It's why he stayed away from family, or anyone who knew them.

"You've had a lot of strikes, some deserving, some

not so much," Zeke said. "Rocky and Ethan are like brothers. I'd do anything for them. I also know they can be judgmental pricks when it comes to you."

"Excuse me?" This was an unexpected turn of events and Weston wasn't sure if he could trust it, much less know what to think. Zeke wasn't his friend. Currently, he was his boss and his loyalty belonged to Weston's cousins.

"There are two sides to a coin and two sides to every story. I'm sure there are gaps in what they think they know and I'm willing to give you the benefit of the doubt with some things, with some exceptions." He held up two fingers. "The first one is an incident with some ex-girlfriend and the second is your dishonorable discharge. I can't see past either of those things until you show me you're not that man."

Weston squared his shoulders and reined in his anger. "I can understand why you'd take issue with both those things. I once tried to explain what really happened in regard to my ex, but it fell on deaf ears."

"Are you denying it happened?"

"It's a complicated story and if you ever want to hear it, I'm happy to tell it. My cousins' version is tainted because they don't know the entire truth. Only my reaction to what happened, which is bad, I will admit. But the discharge?" He let out a long breath. "It's under review." He walked a fine line by telling Zeke, but he needed to make an ally not an enemy and eventually, he'd have to tell his cousins about the review board anyway.

"You've applied to have it overturned?"

"I don't want to go back to the Army. That's done. But I'm in the process of appealing the dishonorable portion of my discharge." This was a piece of information that he hadn't told anyone in his family. When he tried to tell his parents, they didn't want to hear it. When he called his cousins, they didn't want to know the details. They begrudgingly gave him a job and told him the Army didn't make mistakes.

But this time they had and he was going to prove it with the help of Special Agent Fenmore Harley.

"I'd appreciate it if you didn't tell my cousins that," Weston added.

"Why not?"

"I have a lot to prove and they will look at that as me doing my damndest to shift blame instead of taking responsibility for happened on my last mission. Besides, it's a long process and the federal agent working on it said it could take months. All I want to do now is focus on regaining the trust of my family."

"The only thing I've been told was that your mission blew up and you were dishonorably discharged. What can you tell me about that?"

"Unfortunately, nothing. Besides being classified, I have been instructed to let the system work on my behalf. Until that happens, I'm keeping my nose down, my head held high, and staying out of trouble."

"That's the right attitude." Zeke nodded. "There's a man by the name of Brayden Gibson who works with search and rescue."

"I know who Brayden is. He's been friends with Ethan for a long time."

"You should give him a call. He went through a lot before moving here and he might be a good sounding board. He's not family, and he's not me." Zeke jerked his thumb over his shoulder. "And he's not Haven. She has her own shit to deal with and she's too sweet of a girl to say no to someone else."

"Understood."

"Finish up this stack of dishes and when you're done, come out to the bar. I need to run a quick errand. I hope you really do know your way around a few mixed drinks."

"I bartended on and off for a buddy for years. I can handle it." Weston took the tray and started sorting, doing his best to put what happened to Eric out of his mind. He'd lost half his team on that mission. While he knew deep down it was a fucked-up assignment destined to fail thanks to an asshole, a corrupted CIA agent in charge of the JSOC (Joint Special Operations Command) team, he couldn't help but wonder if he'd done one thing differently, would his best friend still be alive?

CHAPTER TWO

Haven Taylor leaned against the bar. Her feet throbbed and her bones ached. She was grateful for the extra shifts Zeke tossed her way. Lord knew she needed the money. She hoped to have enough saved to start classes in the fall. It would only be part-time, but she needed a few more pennies in the bank to feel comfortable doing that. At least that was the excuse she told herself. The idea of returning to college sent her heart pounding. "You're pretty good at being a bartender." She soaked in the handsome newcomer's sexy swagger. A mixture of contradicting emotions zoomed through her body. They landed in her belly and wrestled about like two toddlers arguing over a favorite toy.

Physical attraction wasn't a luxury she could

afford. The sensations were confusing. The fear of what could happen if she acted on them had a death grip on her soul. And yet she soaked in Weston like he was a ray of sunshine.

He looked more like his cousin Ethan than Rocky with his defined cheekbones, although he did have a five o'clock shadow that if he let grow, might give him that rugged look that Rocky sported. But it was his deep soulful eyes that drew her in like a hypnotist. They were kind and sensitive, but a heaviness lurked in the shadows.

She had avoided men since she'd returned to Fallport, and for good reason. Those who knew her past wanted something from her and they made their intentions clear. Those that didn't learned her history quickly, making her life awkward and uncomfortable. Part of her wanted to run, but this sleepy little town offered her protection, something she desperately needed.

"Thanks." Weston smiled.

"Where'd you learn about mixing drinks?"

"A buddy of mine had a family restaurant. When we were stationed near his hometown, I sometimes worked there."

"Where is he now?"

Weston's face hardened and his brown eyes turned smoky. She'd seen that look before.

She reached across the bar and rested her hand over Weston's. "I'm sorry," she whispered.

"For what?" He blinked.

"I shouldn't assume, but I'm guessing your friend isn't with us anymore."

Weston tapped his knuckles on the wood counter. "That's not something I either like to discuss or dwell on."

Zeke stepped from the kitchen. "I'll be back in an hour. The kitchen is closed. When I return, we can shut this place down."

"We can handle it if you want to go home for the night," Haven said. "Can't we, Weston."

"I'm not sure Zeke's ready to task me with that responsibility." Weston wiped down the bar with a little more gusto than needed.

"That would actually be helpful," Zeke said. "It's midnight. I doubt anyone else is coming in, so once these few cash out, you two can close up."

"Thanks for the vote of confidence." Weston nodded.

"It's her who gets that." Zeke kissed Haven's cheek. "Don't hesitate to call me if you need anything at all." He strolled out of the bar, glancing once over his shoulder, giving Weston quite the glare.

"Pay him no mind. He thinks every new guy who walks in here is hitting on me and he doesn't believe most men are good enough."

"He's probably right." Weston winked. "On both accounts."

"Oh my gosh. Are you flirting?"

"Absolutely not." Weston raised a finger. "However, you are a beautiful woman who is incredibly sweet and way too kind. You should be careful. Men in bars always get the wrong impression."

He was right and that pissed her off for different reasons. "Wonderful. Do I now have another overprotective ex-military guy who's going to get all brotherly on my hands?"

He pointed. "I think they'd like their check."

"Saved by the customer." She turned and scurried off toward a table full of young ladies having a fun night out in a small town. Part of her hated this job. It reminded her of everything she'd done wrong in her short life. When Zeke had first offered it to her, she'd turned it down. The last thing she wanted to do was serve drinks to a bunch of drunk people, especially men. She'd had enough groping to last a lifetime.

While she had skills, she'd dropped out of college halfway through her third year. She'd given her life to an asshole who controlled everything she did, including continuing to send her out on escort jobs to his high-rolling friends. When she finally left, her parents had become so ashamed, they wanted nothing to do with her and still didn't. Even two months after her return to Fallport, if they saw her walking down the street, they looked the other way.

They went as far as to blackball her, making it impossible for her to get an office job with her father's contacts, leaving her with one prospect.

Zeke.

The good news was the damn job had given her confidence. It had shown her that she was stronger than she thought. It also gave her built-in protection. She was never alone, although it surprised her that Zeke had left tonight. That almost never happened, and while she knew nothing about Weston's past, she'd been warned to stay away. She figured either he was a womanizing jerk or he came to Fallport broken.

She suspected it was a bit of both.

"Thank you, ladies. This is very kind and generous of you." She took the cash and slipped it into her apron. "You have a safe night, ya hear."

"You too, Haven," one of the girls said. "See you next time."

Haven returned to the bar. "Looks like that's it," she said. "Why don't I take this tray back to the kitchen while you finish cleaning around the bar." She curled her fingers around the tray and turned.

She gasped, releasing her grip. The glasses crashed to the floor. Her pulse pounded in her ears.

"Are you okay?" Weston raced around the side of the bar. "Your leg is bleeding. Don't move." He took the towel from over his shoulder and tapped it gently on her skin, but she paid him no mind as she stared at Bradly.

It had been two weeks since he dared to show his face, but that didn't stop the threatening texts or messages. Every time she got one, she brought it to the police. She had an active restraining order. He wasn't supposed to come anywhere near her, but still, the cops couldn't do much. Bradly knew people. Every time she thought she'd rid herself of him, he waltzed right back into her life.

"I'm going to get a broom. Stay put." Weston rose, running his hand up and down her arm. "Hey. What's wrong? You look as if you've just seen a ghost."

"No ghost," Bradly said with a snide smile. "Just an old friend."

"You're not welcome here." She took one step backward. "If Zeke catches you in his bar, all hell will break loose."

"Zeke's not here, and I'm not staying long." Bradly raised his hands. "I just want to talk. You owe me that."

"We have nothing to say to each other."

"That's where you're dead wrong," Bradly said.

"I'm sorry, sir. But we're closed." Weston took a step forward, putting a protective arm in front of her. "I'm going to have to ask you to leave."

"And who the fuck are you?" Bradly tilted his head.

Standing behind Weston, she reached into her pocket and snagged her phone. Pressing her head against his back, she quickly texted Zeke. She hated doing it this late, but she had made a promise to him —and to herself—that if and when Bradly showed up again, she wouldn't make the same mistake she had last time. Dealing with him on her own was dangerous. Calling the police only served to piss him off and he'd never pay the price anyway.

She thought cutting a deal with him would make him go away, but it hadn't. The little book she'd taken was the only leverage she had over him and if she gave it back, she'd be toast. Giving it to the authorities wouldn't gain her freedom; it would put her six feet under. No one knew she had it. Not Zeke and his crew. Bradly suspected, though he couldn't prove it, nor would she let him know. As long as it wasn't in Bradly's hands, she believed she'd be safe. That he wouldn't kill her because he'd worry if and when that book would surface.

However, once he had it, all bets were off.

"The man telling you to leave," Weston said.

"You have no authority over me. Now if you don't mind. Haven and I have some unfinished business." Bradly boldly stepped closer.

Weston inched back, crunching the glass under his feet. "This is the last time I'm going to ask you nicely."

"Are you threatening me?" Bradly asked.

"Just do us all a favor and turn around and leave. That way I won't have to forcibly push you through that door." Weston's tone was level and calm, but there was a bite to his words that made Haven shiver.

"This doesn't concern you, whoever the fuck you are," Bradly said. "Haven. This is getting ridiculous. I'm tired of playing this game. Come on. Let's go."

"I'm not going anywhere with you. Not now. Not ever," she said with as much conviction as she could manage.

"You have something that belongs to me, so yes, you are." Bradly lunged forward, doing his best to shove Weston out of the way.

Weston pushed her as he grabbed Bradly by the arm, twisting it behind his back and thrusting his body against the bar. "I warned you."

"You fucking asshole. You have no idea who you're messing with." Bradly turned, swinging his free arm, cocking a fist, hurling it toward Weston's face.

Haven gasped, covering her mouth, stumbling back into a table, knocking over a few chairs.

Weston ducked, dodging the punch. He tackled Bradly to the floor, pressing his face to the hardwood. "You fucked with the wrong man." He hoisted Bradly to his feet, holding both his hands behind his back.

The front door opened. Zeke and Rocky came storming into the room.

"If I ever see you in this bar or near Haven again, you'll live to regret it." Weston hauled Bradly past Zeke and Rocky, shoving him to the curb. "That's not a threat. It's a promise. Now, fuck off." He pulled the door closed, locked it, and leaned against the wood frame. "Who the hell was that guy?"

"A complete douchebag," Rocky said, racing to Haven's side. "Are you okay?"

"I'm fine, thanks to Weston." She let out a long breath.

"I shouldn't have left you." Zeke pulled her in for a big brotherly hug. "I should have known that his silence these last few days didn't mean anything."

"Did he hurt you?" Rocky asked.

She shook her head. "Weston didn't let him get anywhere near me."

Weston hobbled to the closest chair and sat down. He tugged at a piece of glass wedged in his foot before kicking off his shoe and rolling down his sock.

"I'll get the first aid kit," she said.

"It's nothing. Just a small cut." He winced.

Rocky leaned over. "You might need stitches."

"If there's superglue around this joint, that will work just as good."

"Seriously?" Haven paused, glancing over her shoulder. "I can't imagine that's sanitary, much less safe."

"Not the first time I've used it," Weston said.

Haven scurried toward the kitchen and pulled

open the pantry. Snagging the first aid kit, she raced back into the main room, every muscle in her body shaking. "Why don't you let me clean it first?" All she wanted to do was focus on anything other than what just happened.

"Thanks, but I can handle it." Weston took the kit from her hands and smiled. "I've been injured much worse. This is a walk in the park." He pulled out the antiseptic and poured it over a gauze pad. Pressing it on the open wound, he closed his eyes and groaned.

"When was the last time you heard from Bradly?" Rocky asked.

"Two days ago. Same bullshit as always. He says he wants to talk, but we all know he wants me back." She plopped herself in the chair next to Weston, examining his foot. The bleeding had slowed to a trickle as he pinched the skin, dabbing the glue on it and holding it together while the tacky goop took hold. "I didn't respond."

"Who is he to you?" Weston asked.

"The biggest mistake of my life," she muttered. She swallowed. The bitter taste of shame landed in the center of her gut.

"I've texted Lewis. He'll up the patrols by your apartment and the bar over the next few days until we know Bradly crawled back under his rock," Rocky said. "He will eventually give up."

"We all know that's not true." Haven folded her hands in her lap, clasping tightly.

"Not to keep beating a dead horse, but that's in part because you went back to him twice. He believes he can break you down. That it's only a matter of time." Zeke leaned against the bar with his arms folded. "It's not a judgment, it's just a fact."

"I'm lucky I got away the last time." Haven rubbed her cheek.

Rocky squeezed her shoulder. "He looks at you like property."

"Not to mention he believes you have information that could hurt his business." Zeke arched a brow.

"I'm not going to give the police names." She crossed her arms. "It won't help. You know what he's capable of."

"I'm a little lost in this conversation," Weston said. "Does anyone want to clue me in?"

"It's nothing you need to worry about." Rocky strolled to the front window and peered through the glass.

"We should read him in," Zeke said. "I'm short-handed and I can't be here all the time. Weston can help protect her both here and at her apartment since he now lives in the same building."

A warm tingle slid down her spine. She sat up a little taller. Having someone like Weston in her building did ease her fears. She hadn't gotten a good night's sleep since Bradly kicked the shit out of her right before she fled the last time.

Rocky turned. "Are you okay with that?" He held her stare. "With Weston helping to protect you?"

Anger filled her soul. Everyone in Fallport knew about her sordid past and no one except Ethan, Rocky, Zeke, and the rest of the crew with the search and rescue team understood why or how it happened. Most citizens of Fallport viewed her as the predator, not the victim. They believed she'd been a criminal and her own parents couldn't even look at her.

She understood that she made a poor choice when she went to work for the escort agency, but that didn't mean she deserved what Bradly had done.

"I don't like having to have any of you watch over me, but I know what Bradly's capable of. However, I don't want to put anyone out," she said.

"I'm happy to help keep an eye out for that asshole and keep you safe." Weston reached across the table and squeezed her hand. "You don't have to give me the reasons why if you don't want to."

"He should know a few things," Zeke said. "Mostly that where Bradly comes from, he has cops, judges, the mayor, and fancy lawyers in his pocket."

"Not to mention a few criminals that make terrorists look like nice little old ladies." Rocky rubbed the back of his neck. "We've spent the last two months trying to find his blind spot and haven't been successful."

"Whatever you all need me to do, I've got your backs," Weston said.

"Working all the same shifts as Haven so that she's never alone here or at her apartment would be a good start." Zeke nodded.

"It means you might not start right away with search and rescue." Rocky cocked his head.

"I'm here to make myself useful." Weston pulled his bloody sock over his bandaged foot. "Put me to work in whatever capacity necessary."

"We appreciate that, man." Zeke slapped his shoulder. "You can start by making sure she gets home safe and bringing her back here at noon. You're both working a double."

Weston jumped to his feet. "Consider it done."

"This is the part where I throw a small temper

tantrum." Haven planted her hands on her hips and glared. "Am I supposed to live the rest of my life in fear?"

"Until that asshole is behind bars, yes." Rocky glared. "We're lucky that Weston understood the threat and tossed that fucker out on his ass. We're even luckier that nothing worse happened considering my cousin has a temper and Bradly can be a violent man."

Haven didn't need to be reminded, but she honestly wanted clarification regarding Weston. But this wasn't the time or place. And she wasn't about to ask Zeke and especially not Rocky.

The tension between Rocky and Weston was palpable.

"I will be forever grateful to all of you, but I can't keep living like this." She fought the tears that threatened to break free. "I'm getting tired of being afraid and constantly looking over my shoulder." If she gave the book back, she'd be dead. Even if she did it anonymously because no one walked away from Bradly.

No one.

"I might not know the situation. However, I do know that my cousins are damn good at what they do and that sometimes these things take time. This won't be forever. But until they can find a way to make sure he can't come after you ever again, I suggest you let them protect you the best way they know how." Weston groaned as he raised his leg and wiggled his foot.

"I should have never come back here." She reorganized the first aid kit.

"Running isn't the answer either," Rocky said. "I didn't notice your car here."

"That's because I walked." She narrowed her eyes. "It's only a mile."

"Weston will drive you home," Zeke said. "Why don't you go grab your stuff."

"There are a few things I need to do in the back before leaving." She turned on her heel and stormed off toward the kitchen. She wasn't angry with any of them, but at the situation.

And herself.

She had no one else to blame. She'd been the one to take the job with the escort agency to begin with. Her one friend had told her that sex was never part of the equation and for the first six months, that had been true. All her clients were rich, powerful men who wanted a pretty young thing to dress up their arm at some event for the evening. Her role had been to look sexy, smile, and occasionally say something smart and sweet.

Everything changed when she met Bradly. It didn't happen overnight, but slowly, he took control of her life, and he was still making it a living hell.

WESTON SWEPT the floor and dumped the glass in the garbage while he tried to make sense of the evening's events, which was impossible with the little information he had.

"I'm not going to ask a bunch of questions about the situation, but I think I should mention something," Weston said.

"And what's that?" Rocky asked.

"When Bradly was here, he mentioned she has something that belongs to him."

Rocky and Zeke exchanged glances.

"You don't have to tell me what that means, but it seemed to me that's what he was after." Weston squared his shoulders.

"She swears she doesn't have anything more than information in her head, but honestly, neither one of us believe her," Zeke said. "Bradly's connections are far and wide. Bringing him down is not an easy task."

"If it was, we would have done it already." Rocky fingered his beard. "We've pushed her a few times to hand over whatever she has and she tripped up once, telling me that the only thing she has will put her and the rest of the girls in danger. She's not willing to do that."

"Girls?" Weston didn't like the sound of that.

"We can't prove anything. The two times Bradly was arrested, the charges were dropped the next morning because he has incredibly powerful people who want his services."

Weston glanced over his shoulder. A picture of what might have been going on in Haven's life had formed and he didn't like it. "One thing I've learned from all my past mistakes in life is keeping information only gives people power to either believe the wrong things or to put you in the worst position possible."

"Those are wise words, coming from you." Rocky cocked his head. "You're not allowed to carry, are you?"

Fuck. By answering truthfully, he'd have to explain a few things and he wasn't prepared to go into detail with his cousin. However, the situation might require it and based on what he'd just said, he might as well dig into the truth. He handed the broom to Zeke. "I was granted a permit, temporarily, while my case is under review." He held Rocky's stare. This had been his entire reason for coming to Fallport. To make things right. If he could mend fences with his cousins, he might be able to do it with the rest of his family. He missed them terribly and desperately needed them. He was tired of going through life alone. It stopped now.

"You're talking about your dishonorable discharge?" Rocky arched a brow. "You instigated a review?"

"A federal agent initiated it." Weston had promised himself that he would do his best to be honest with his cousins. Even concerning his discharge—if they honestly wanted to know. However, Fenmore had told him not to get his hopes up. She had her work cut out to prove where the original board had gone wrong, not to mention the CIA agent on the mission. She also advised him it was in his best interest to keep the details of her inquisition to himself. The fewer people who knew what she was doing, the better.

Fucking Phil Wicker. This whole goddamned

thing was his fault. He was a traitor to his country and a total asshole. But Weston couldn't prove it.

No matter what Weston had been through regarding his cousins, or his family, he knew without a shadow of a doubt and when it came to this, he could trust them. He had to if he wanted to keep his job and have any chance at a new life.

Only, he thought he'd be able wait until Fenmore had what she needed and his dishonorable portion of his discharge had been changed before telling this tale.

"I'm curious as to why?" Rocky asked with a less combative tone for a change.

"There's a lot I can't tell you because the mission is classified and—"

"Tell us what you can." Rocky waved his hand in front of a table and took a seat. "I honestly want to know."

"To make a very long story short..." Weston hobbled closer, easing his ass on the chair. "My team got bad intel, and we were ambushed. Three of us pushed back, but we followed through with the order given by the CIA agent on the ground who was in charge of the JSOC mission. We had a bad feeling about the change in plans based on the new information this agent got. Something was off, but we couldn't put our finger on it. Four good men died. The other two who agreed with me were killed during the fight."

"Eric Dobson was one of them." Rocky lowered his chin. "I was saddened to hear about his death."

Weston swallowed. Hard. Eric had died in his arms. It had been the single worst moment in his life. "I was shot three times trying to prevent that from happening." He lifted his shirt, showing off two scars where the bullets had torn through his body, nearly ending his life. A juicy piece of information that he wasn't sure anyone in his family cared to pay attention to.

"We knew you'd been wounded, but no one said how bad." Rocky let out a long breath. "And before we get into an argument about our inability to reach out, you didn't communicate well either."

"That's fair," Weston said. "I spent three weeks in a hospital in Germany. During the end of my stay, I was essentially arrested for disobeying a direct order, which was bullshit." He held up his hand. "I questioned it. I asked for clarification and wanted to speak to the JSOC commander stateside, but the CIA agent told us there wasn't time. We had to move, so we did."

"What you're saying is you believe the agent set you up," Zeke said. "But why would he do that?"

"Special Agent Fenmore Harley, who's taken on my case, informed me that this particular CIA agent has been on her radar for some time and this isn't the first time it's happened." Weston felt a sense of relief telling the story, but especially to his cousin. It was an odd sensation. Growing up, he'd wanted their approval. As an adult, he resented their judgment. Right now, all he desired was the opportunity to start fresh. To be part of a family again. "She didn't like how my case went so quickly in front of a board she was pushed off of and once a new department head was named in her office, she was given the go-ahead to take on my case. For the record, she contacted me."

"Who's the CIA Agent?" Zeke asked.

"Fenmore doesn't want me to get into the specifics of the case, so I don't think it's wise I say his name out loud. She believes it will hurt me if I do."

"Was it Phil Wicker?" Rocky arched a brow. "Please tell me it wasn't that fucking prick."

Weston's heart thumped in the center of his throat. He tried swallowing but couldn't manage the action. He stared at his cousin, unable to shift his gaze.

"Fuck me," Zeke mumbled. "I hate that guy."

"You and me both." Rocky nodded. "I was hoping to never hear that man's name again."

"How the hell do you know Wicker?" Weston finally got his voice back.

"I crossed paths with him about a year before leaving the military. He's a cocky, self-centered prick who nearly ruined an op." Rocky slammed his fist on the table. "Did he know we're cousins?"

"Your name never came up, but a lot of people I worked with in JSOC knew we're related. It was like it was tattooed on my forehead or something." Weston rubbed the back of his neck. "You don't think he came after me specifically because he's got a beef with you?"

"That's exactly what I believe." Rocky nodded. "And he has one with Ethan and Zeke as well."

"Not to mention he had a run-in with Brayden five years ago," Zeke said. "The guy's a loose cannon and he's about as crooked as they come. I can't believe he's running JSOC ops. When we knew him, he was doing intelligence."

"On my mission he was on the ground with us, but thank God he was there as support only." Rocky ran his fingers through his beard. "He loved using the phrase, *you're on a need to know basis and right now, you don't need to know.* Fucking pissed me off, man."

"He does love to say those words." Weston let out a dry laugh.

"I want to speak with this FBI agent. We all might have information that can help your case when it comes to that fucker." Rocky stood, resting a hand on Weston's shoulder and squeezing. It was a brotherly sensation and something Weston hadn't ever expected from his cousin.

"What kind of intel?" Weston asked.

"I believe he tried to sabotage my mission. I brought it to my superiors. There was a case review and he was reprimanded. Our paths never crossed again professionally, but the few times I ran into him, he made it perfectly clear that someday I'd pay for what I did to his career," Rocky said.

"Obviously, whatever happened didn't stick. He runs ops with JSOC and has a lot of power. Too much if you ask me." Weston threaded his fingers through his hair. "He was our contact on the ground and we took orders from him. It sucked. Eric didn't trust him as far as he could spit. He tried to get confirmation from someone else higher up. Our CO told us it was a JSOC mission run through the CIA.

It was Wicker and this guy Walter Mathis. Eric never did get through and we had no other choice but to follow orders. We were fucked either way."

"Your special agent is onto him, so that's something," Zeke said. "Do you know if there's a reason outside of your case for her wanting to take him down?"

"I got the impression it's bigger than Wicker, but she didn't say." Weston had questioned Fenmore on her interest and she had mentioned a different case she'd been working on that had to do with a different JSOC team. All she'd give him was there was a connection between Wicker and another person in the CIA. His best guess was Mathis.

"What's her job, exactly?" Rocky asked.

"She reviews military discharges and votes on courses of action. She was not on my initial review board and mentioned the whole thing stank. She believes she can overturn the dishonorable and at least reverse it to a general at the worst."

"And at best?"

"An honorable, but I'd be happy to just have the dishonorable removed. I deserve a lot of things, but that's not one of them," Weston admitted. "To be totally honest, the thing with Darlene came back and bit me in the ass during the hearing. It was used against me to show that I'm violent and struggle with authority, but according to Fenmore, that should have been irrelevant and never brought to the review board's attention."

"Not to be an asshole, but shit did happen. You did fuck up."

Weston closed his eyes and counted to ten. He blinked. "I take full responsibility for *my* actions. I went to anger management and I cleaned up my act. But there are things you don't know. Things that she and Ted… it doesn't matter. I'm not the same person I was at twenty-two and it's not related to what happened in South America."

"I would like to know your side of the Darlene story, but we can do that another time," Rocky said.

Weston blew out a puff of air. No one had ever asked before, except for the judge, who showed him mercy, but still held him accountable. Something that Weston would be forever grateful for. He needed understanding as much as he needed a swift kick in the ass. "It's not an easy story to tell," he admitted. "There are a lot of things I'm ashamed of during that time in my life. I used poor judgment and I don't want to make excuses, so if and when we do have that conversation, you'll need to understand that my side isn't about that, but truth."

"Perhaps I may have partially misjudged you," Rocky said. "However, you have never given me or anyone in this family any reason to think otherwise."

Now was not the time to remind his cousin how often he'd chosen to ignore Weston. Or to tell him the truth. "Like I said, I've made bad decisions and paid the price."

Rocky nodded. "Make sure you have your weapon on you at all times and don't leave Haven's side. Bradly is a dangerous man. When he does show his face, try not to engage. Call the sheriff and contact us immediately."

"I need to ask you something." Weston rose. He and his cousin were almost exactly the same height, but Rocky carried a good thirty pounds more of solid muscles. He was an impressive man and Weston wouldn't want to go even one round with Rocky because he'd lose.

"What's that?" Rocky squared his shoulders.

"You placed me in this bar. You found me an apartment. I had originally thought it was because you wanted to keep an eye on me and control me. Now I'm wondering if all that had to do with protecting Haven," Weston said.

"A little bit of both, but mostly the latter." Rocky glanced over his shoulder. "Bradly tried kidnapping her. He almost succeeded a month ago and we thought we had him. Sheriff Bob Lewis even arrested him, but all those charges ended up being tossed out. Bradly found a way to make it look like entrapment and harassment. Technically, Ethan, Zeke, and I aren't supposed to be within one hundred feet of him."

"Are you serious? How is that even legal?" Weston asked.

"I might have hit him," Zeke said. "Rocky's weapon might have accidentally discharged, missing his feet by a few inches. He feels threatened by us."

"He should." Weston laughed. "And you're worried about my temper?"

"That's kind of why we want you there." Rocky cocked his head. "Just don't go and get yourself arrested."

"I don't plan on it," Weston said. "Where is my apartment in relation to hers?"

"There are only two on each floor. You're right next to her." Rocky patted his shoulder. "But she's off-limits. You've developed quite the reputation for being—"

"That was a long time ago." Weston let out a long breath. "I'm also not looking for any entanglements at the moment. My focus is on getting my shit together." He'd made a ton of mistakes after Darlene had broken his heart, and one of them had been to screw any woman who gave him attention. He hurt too many girls in the process—something he regretted.

"All right." Rocky nodded. "To be safe, I'll follow you and Haven home and help you do a perimeter check. Whenever Bradly pays her a visit, he doesn't go away quietly."

"Sounds like a plan." Looked like Weston was on protection detail. At least he was doing something more than bussing tables.

CHAPTER THREE

Haven stepped from her bedroom. She'd spent the night tossing and turning, mostly out of fear. But then there was Weston who had insisted on sleeping on her sofa, with her damn dog. Fucking traitor. Gunner didn't like most people. American bulldogs were notorious for being loyal to their owners, which is why she rescued the stupid dog.

And Gunner had been a good watch dog for the last four months. He barked at everything and growled at anyone who came close, except Weston.

Gunner tolerated Zeke and Brayden. He accepted Ethan, Rocky, and some of the other men at search and rescue, but for the most part, Gunner was there to protect her, and right now, he was lying at Weston's feet, licking his toes, looking like a pathetic puppy.

She sighed, wondering if Weston stayed at her place at the request of Zeke, or if Weston had decided that one all on his own. She appreciated his diligence to her safety and his kindness. But there was a deep sadness in the man's soul. It reached into her heart. She could only imagine what had put that kind of pain in his eyes.

"You're up early." He leaned against the kitchen counter in sweatpants and a dark T-shirt, holding a tall mug. Gunner yawned, thumping his tail, but didn't move. Normally, when he saw Haven, he'd go nuts, leaping to his hind legs to greet her, but not this morning.

Weston leaned over and patted the dog's head. He hadn't said much since they returned to her apartment last night. He checked the building, collected a few things from his place, and made himself comfortable on her sofa. He mentioned he'd be going outside a few times through the evening to make sure Bradly wasn't anywhere to be found.

She told him Bradly would show up and then wait a day or two before making another move. He knew she was surrounded by a bunch of highly decorated ex-military men. Bradly wasn't stupid and could be patient when it served his purpose. He told her she wouldn't last a month without him—it had been two.

He'd tried sending a couple of the other girls to have a friendly chat, but they weren't friendly at all. They were warnings about what would happen to them and her if she didn't return. Zeke made it perfectly clear that she couldn't save the world and that those other women weren't her responsibility. However, that didn't change the guilt that swirled around in her belly. Or the fear that Bradly would harm those girls.

"I got tired of staring at the ceiling fan." She pulled open the cupboard and pulled out a mug, placing it under the coffee maker. Lifting the top, she inserted a fresh pod and hit the largest setting. "And I missed my dog."

Weston pulled out a chair and straddled it, setting his coffee on the kitchen table. Gunner scooted across the floor, plopping his head right back on Weston's feet.

Weston chuckled. "I don't know what to tell you about Gunner. I tried to shoo him back to your bedroom, but every time I got up to go do a perimeter check, he wanted to come. Maybe he knows something's up."

"He doesn't like people, so this is weird." She shook her head.

"Well, I don't either and if it makes you feel better, there has been no sighting of Bradly."

"Oh, he's out there." She pulled her cell from her pocket. "He texted me about an hour ago, asking to meet for breakfast. I ignored it, which will make him angry."

"We should text that to Zeke and the rest of the gang."

"I already did."

Weston rubbed his chin. "Can you include me in on those communications from now on?"

She nodded. "Sorry, I should have done that."

"Have any of them responded?"

"They are going to grab a bite to eat there this morning. That should be interesting."

"Yeah. I wouldn't mind being a fly on that wall," Weston said. "I know this is none of my business, but what does Bradly want?"

"Me," she said.

"You don't have to answer, but why?"

The machine gurgled as it spit out the last drop. She lifted the mug and blew before tasting that first delicious sip while she contemplated what version of the story she might tell Weston. Someone in town would eventually whisper the rumors and half-truths in his ear. Everyone had an opinion about what she'd been doing. Most people glared at her with disdain.

Few felt sorry for her, but ultimately blamed her for her own misery.

There were a couple people at search and rescue who questioned her job choice and wondered how she didn't know what she'd gotten herself into. They saw her as this smart girl with a bright future. They didn't understand how vulnerable she'd been or how Bradly's charm had lured her into a life of crime.

"That's a difficult question." She snagged the pastries she'd bought yesterday from the pantry and set them on the table. She pulled out one of the chocolate ones and picked at it. "I suppose you could say he was my boyfriend and it was an abusive relationship."

"I mean no disrespect, but how old are you and what's the age difference there?"

"I'm twenty-five. Bradly's forty-two."

"Damn. That's seventeen years. I thought I was old at thirty-five." He lifted his hand. "I'm not judging. Just making an observation."

"Trust me. I get judged for that all the time, among other things."

"Are you referencing the abuse? Because no one should put that on you. It's not your fault. That's all on Bradly."

If Weston knew the half of it, he might feel differently. Haven had gone out on one date since returning to Fallport. She had wanted to try to put the past behind her by being normal. She thought Tyler was different. He acted as if nothing in her past could scare him off. He seemed like a nice guy and she desperately wanted to pretend the last few years hadn't happened.

She believed having a decent man in her life might give her some respect in the community. But the second he learned the sordid, ugly details of her past, he ran for the hills as fast as he could. He quit his job at Zeke's and was currently dating someone more respectable. His words, not hers, and that stung.

"Knowing that and believing it are often two different things," she said.

"No one deserves to be abused and unfortunately, the abuser often finds ways to gaslight their victim into believing it was all their fault." He reached out and took her hand. "It takes time to get that shit out of your head, but you will." A vibrating noise caught her attention.

He reached behind him and snagged his phone from the counter. "It's Zeke. He's at the diner and so is Bradly. I guess Bradly decided to call the sheriff, citing the restraining order. Zeke's concerned it could be a decoy and I need to be on high alert." He reached down and scratched Gunner's butt. "You hear that, Gunn Gunn. We need to be prepared for the worst-case scenario."

"I seriously don't understand my dog. He doesn't like men, which is why I got him. Zeke has to bribe him with treats to get into this apartment when I'm not home."

"Are you trying to tell me he's afraid of this sweet creature?" Weston leaned over and kissed Gunner's nose.

The dog responded by lapping the man's face.

"Utterly terrified of him, but they have come to an understanding." She laughed. "You seem to have already developed some weird cosmic bond."

"Well, I've always had a love for dogs. I worked in a vet's office when I was sixteen. My ex-fiancée was in veterinarian school when we were together. At one time we had four dogs, five cats, and a fucking pig of all things."

"A pig? That had to be interesting."

"That was one animal I didn't get along with, but

I always told myself that if I ever left the Army and settled in one spot, I'd get a dog and cat. My studio right now doesn't appear to be big enough for both so I might start with a kitten."

"Yeah. This building has a studio and a one-bedroom on each floor. You got the short end of the stick. And I would have never pegged you for a cat person."

He chuckled. "I love the furry little creatures." He lifted his cell. "Zeke and my cousins are sitting outside the diner. Bradly is still inside. They want us to stay put until it's time for our—"

Ding. Dong.

Gunner jumped to his feet. His tail dove between his legs as he raced to the door, growling and barking in a deep menacing voice. He had a fierce sound that should scare anyone who dared to enter her building.

"Quiet." She rose, smoothing down the front of her jeans.

"Are you expecting anyone?"

"No." She made her way to the intercom. "Hello?"

"Hey, Haven. It's Zelda. How are you?"

Haven froze with her finger hovering over the button.

"Who's Zelda?"

"Someone I used to know when I lived in Fairfax. She's friendly with Bradly." That was the understatement of the year. Zelda was one of his girls. The worst part was Haven had—for lack of a better word—recruited her, something that weighed heavily in her heart.

"Find out what she wants." Weston stood. He picked up his cell and tapped at the screen.

"What are you doing here?" Haven asked. She sucked in a deep, slow breath. The last time Bradly sent someone, it had been Amanda, her ex-roommate and the woman who had brought her into the fold.

"I came to warn you," Zelda said.

Bullshit.

"Please. Let me in. I only have a few moments." Zelda's voice crackled through the intercom.

"Do it. I'll be hiding in the bedroom." Weston nodded. "Keep Gunner with you. If you feel unsafe or need me to show my face, tell her you need to take the dog outside. That will be my cue to come out of the woodwork."

Haven swallowed as she pressed the button. "Come on up."

Weston squeezed her biceps. "If you get really spooked, just call my name. I'll be listening."

"Thanks." She snagged the leash and hooked it to Gunner's collar. The dog might prefer women to men, but he could still get snarly around strangers. She sucked in a deep breath as she pressed the call button. "I'll buzz you in. I'm on the fourth floor. Apartment 4A." She unlocked the door. "Be a good boy, Gunner. No jumping."

Gunner whined, glancing up at her with a tilted head.

"Sit."

The dog did as commanded.

There was no elevator in the building. Haven waited with her heart beating frantically in her chest.

The top of Zelda's head appeared as she climbed the last flight of stairs.

Gunner barked twice.

"Quiet."

"Does he or she bite?" Zelda stopped three steps from the top, gripping the railing.

"I wouldn't pet him," Haven said. "What are you doing here and don't give me this bullshit it's to warn me. I know better."

"Can I come in for a minute?"

"I guess." Haven tugged at Gunner's leash, leading him to his doggie bed. "Lie down and stay." She leaned over and patted the dog's back. "I know Bradly's here and that means you came with him."

"Of course I did." Zelda set her purse on the coffee table. She wore a stunning yellow dress with tiny straps, showing off her shoulders and highlighting her fantastic new breasts. "And he's pissed you sent your goons to the restaurant instead of meeting him. All he wants to do is talk."

"You know that's not true." There had been no love lost between Haven and Zelda. There had been a fair amount of jealousy on Zelda's part. She had wanted to be Bradly's number one girl and now she had that chance, but Haven knew that came at a price.

A big one.

She wondered if Zelda had already started paying it.

"You left with his property and he wants it back. That's all," Zelda said.

Haven laughed. "He thinks that property is me and I want nothing to do with him, his world, or you for that matter. I won't be bullied anymore."

Gracefully, Zelda lowered herself into the chair by the mantel. She crossed her tanned, toned legs. She sported three-inch heels that matched her dress. Bradly always expected his girls to look their best and wear designer clothing only. Zelda had come from little to no money, much like Haven. She had struggled to pay for school and needed extra cash. Exactly the kind of girl that Bradly preyed on. He offered her solutions and stole her soul in the process.

The worst part was Haven had handed Zelda to Bradly on a silver platter.

"I tried to warn you about him when I left," Haven said quietly. "I told you the kind of man he was, but you didn't want to listen."

"You're the one who introduced me to him. Got me the job." Zelda raised her fingers, looking at her pretty manicured nails. "I don't understand what your problem is. You hurt Bradly and the rest of us." Zelda slowly rose, smoothing down her dress. "He knows you have the book. Give it to me and he'll let you go."

"I don't know what you're talking about."

"He's done being nice. All you have to do is hand it over and we'll leave you alone forever. If you don't…" Zelda shrugged. "Consider yourself warned. You know the consequences for going against Bradly."

"Hey, babe. Have you seen my keys? I can't find them anywhere." Weston strolled out of the bedroom wearing boxers and a T-shirt. It was hard not to look him up and down and admire his swagger and audacity. Gunner immediately jumped to his feet with his tail wagging like crazy. Weston bent over and greeted the dog like they were best friends. "Good boy," he said. "Oh, sorry. I didn't know we had company." He stretched out his hand. "I'm Weston. And you are?"

"Just leaving." Zelda smiled. "We'll be in town for another night. Remember what I said." She turned. "You know how to reach us. Do the right thing and we can call it even."

Gunner growled.

"Heel," Weston commanded.

Damn dog listened.

Zelda scurried out the door, nearly tripping over her *fuck me* heels.

"I didn't give the code. And what's up with calling me babe? Are you kidding me?" Haven planted her hands on her hips and glared. "Put some freaking clothes on."

"I wanted to send a message to the person who obviously was threatening you that you are not alone."

"Not the right message to send," she mumbled. "The last thing I need is for Bradly to believe I'm sleeping with anyone, but especially someone like you."

"Ouch. That hurt." He tapped the center of his chest. "But I disagree. If Bradly believes a man is staying here all the time with you, he's going to think twice about barging in."

"You don't know Bradly."

"Maybe not. But she didn't come here to warn you. She was here to case out where you live. To see the inside. How easy it might be to gain access. Bradly knew you wouldn't show and that you'd send Zeke or my cousins. Whatever it is they believe you have, they will go to any length to get it."

She opened her mouth, but snapped it closed right quick.

"I'm going to see about making sure someone can watch this place while we're at the bar. Tonight, I'm installing security cameras and changing the locks." He inched closer, taking her chin with his thumb and forefinger. "And if you did take something, bring it with you tonight and please reconsider letting us have a look. It's the only way we can help you. Without full knowledge, we're flying blind."

She stared into his intense gaze. Her heart beat relentlessly in her throat. Her dry eyes burned and her muscles shook.

Weston smoothed his thumb across her cheek. "I know you're scared, but you're playing with fire and it's only going to get worse."

"You don't understand," she whispered. "You don't know the whole story."

"I don't have to." He pressed his lips over hers in a warm, tender kiss. "You can trust me. I know what it's like to be in—"

"You don't have a clue." She pushed him away. "We better get ready for work." She made a beeline for the bedroom. His sensitivity was more than she could take, especially because he had no idea what she'd done. When he did, he'd not only wish he'd never kissed her, but he wouldn't look at her the same way. What man would?

CHAPTER FOUR

There had been many missions in Weston's career where there'd been lapses in the intel. He was often expected to risk his life for the greater good without knowing the exact purpose. He'd be given a directive and was expected to follow it. For the most part, he did it without question.

He sat in the corner booth in the back of the bar with Ethan, Rocky, and Brayden. He had no problem helping Haven, but he wanted answers. He deserved to know the specifics if he was tasked with a protection detail. It might help him do his job better.

Not to mention understand Haven.

His attraction for her grew every minute he spent with her and he was desperate to gain some control. He'd formed various scenarios about her situation and part of him wanted her past to be so sordid that it would squelch the emotions filling his heart. However, he wasn't sure that was possible.

He glanced to his left as she breezed past to wait on a table of young men celebrating one of them getting engaged. Inwardly, he groaned, remembering the day he'd proposed to Darlene. He'd been twenty-one years old. He thought she was the love of his life. The perfect woman. She loved animals and didn't complain about his deployments. It scared her sometimes, but she never once asked him to leave the military.

And she wanted a family, something he had desperately wanted too.

Through therapy, he'd learned he wanted someone to love him back, something he didn't feel he'd gotten from his own family. At the time, he hadn't realized how he'd pushed them all away. He hadn't seen his mistakes. Or the way he'd hurt people in his quest for acceptance. He'd been a dumbass kid trying to prove his worth, and in the process, he'd lost almost everything that mattered.

But Darlene had broken his heart in ways that took years to come back from. To this day, he wasn't sure he could ever trust another woman again. Not completely, anyway.

But he was drawn to Haven in ways he hadn't been in a long time. Her sweetness reached into his soul. She had seen the crueler side of the world, and her eyes showed it. He wanted to help her through whatever had happened, but he didn't have a clue.

"I'm not thrilled with the stunt you pulled this morning," Ethan said.

"It got the point across that Haven won't ever be alone." Weston shifted his gaze. "I need you all to read me in on who the fuck this Bradly dude is and what he really wants."

"Before we get into that," Brayden said. "We wanted to discuss your pending review."

"What about it?" Weston asked.

"I had a long chat with Fenmore." Brayden pushed his beer to the side. "I don't know her personally, but the other case you mentioned that she's working on is someone I do know. A one Captain Darius Ford with the Army. Have you ever heard of him?"

"Actually, I know him. We met about six years ago when I was fresh out of Ranger school on a joint mission. What the hell happened?" Weston asked.

"Can't get into that, except that you and he may have one common denominator. Walter Mathis." Brayden leaned back.

"I don't know him, other than Wicker worked directly under him." Weston shifted. Fenmore had mentioned his name more than once.

"Wicker has a beef with everyone at this table. Walter has one with Darius and everyone on his JSOC team. Fenmore doesn't think the two cases are related in the sense that there is a conspiracy. But she does believe that in both cases, an abuse of power for the sole purpose of revenge has been committed. You…" Brayden tapped his finger on the table. "Are collateral damage in war on us."

"Then Wicker didn't do his homework because until a few weeks ago, the three of us haven't spoken." Rocky shook his head. "Even so, I don't like it when assholes fuck with family. I don't care if I'm speaking to them or not."

"Then where were you when the shit went down with… never mind." Weston thought better of bringing up Darlene. There was no way for them to know. He'd tried to tell everyone the truth, but when no one would even speak to him, he scurried away in shame, his tail between his legs. Darlene chose not to correct people. Ted didn't either. What made that so bad was they moved across the country so they didn't have to deal with the questions. Or the praise for something that wasn't even true.

Assholes.

"We obviously weren't paying attention." Ethan pulled an envelope marked Department of Records from his pocket. "We'll talk about that matter in a second when Brayden is finished."

Westen reached for the document, but his cousin pushed it aside.

Haven strolled up to the table with a bright smile. She had a way about her that made Weston want to forget all about the fact he'd sworn off women. Or that she was completely off-limits, especially if he wanted to live to see another day in this town.

He shouldn't have kissed her, but what was done was done.

"Can I get you guys anything? Another beer or food?" She planted her right hand on her hip and let her left dangle against her thigh. Her long hair had been pulled back into a braid and her sweet eyes sparkled like the Fourth of July.

"I think we're good," Rocky said. "Thanks, Haven."

She stared at Weston. "I don't think you've had anything to eat since breakfast. And you haven't had a break until now, but this doesn't look like one. I'm bringing you a turkey club with a side of potato salad. You're going to eat it and you're going to like it." She waggled her finger in his face. "Understood?"

"Yes, ma'am." His mouth defied his wishes and he smiled like a kid in a candy store.

"It will be up in ten minutes." She turned on her heel and marched toward the kitchen.

Weston glanced between his cousins and swallowed. They both glared at him with death illuminating from their gazes.

Rocky growled.

Ethan flattened his hands on the table. "What the hell was that about?"

"A sandwich," Weston managed, turning to Brayden for help. Weston pleaded with his eyes for backup, but all Brayden did was shrug.

"We told you she was off-limits and you're not following that directive," Ethan said behind a tight jaw.

"Nothing happened, nor will anything. You guys and Haven are the only people I know in this town. We spent a little time talking, so she knows a little about me. And I her. We're friends. That's it. Relax. Jeez." Weston let out a puff of air.

"That better be all that was," Rocky said. "Brayden, could you please go on about the case? We don't have all day."

"Fenmore is making good progress with your situation." Brayden jumped right in where they left off. "The documents and information that she has now regarding what happened to us, but especially me, should be enough to remove the dishonorable part of your discharge."

"Why isn't she telling me this?" Weston asked.

"Because we wanted to," Ethan said. "We immediately believed you fucked up and that assumption was wrong. We'll own our part, but you have to own yours because you let all of us believe a few things about you that weren't true." He tapped his knuckles over the paper. "Why have you let everyone in this family think you're a deadbeat dad who doesn't give two shits about your kid?" He pushed the envelope across the table. "We pulled up the birth records and you're not listed as the father. Ted is. How did that happen?"

"This is my cue to leave.' Brayden slipped from the booth. "I'll see all of you later."

Weston lifted the birth certificate and held it up in his trembling hands. A slew of emotions rattled his nerves. He'd wanted to be Alexandra's father. Part of him still loved that little girl with every fiber of his being. She was thirteen now and he had no contact. He had no idea what she looked like or any idea the kind of young lady she'd become. "Before I answer that, I want to know why you went digging for this."

"You told me there was more to the story," Rocky said. "There's a part of me that still doesn't trust you, so I wanted to find out as much as I could. Uncover the ugly truths. This was one I didn't expect."

"The odd thing about all this is that I've never lied to you." Weston handed his cousin back the document. "But I didn't always tell you everything because I didn't think you'd listen or even believe me."

"We're both here with an open mind, listening," Ethan said. "Are you Alexandra's father?"

"No." Admitting that left a void the size of Texas in Weston's heart.

"How did you find that out?" Rocky asked. "And give us the whole story. We want the experience that we refused to hear fourteen years ago."

"I was so excited when Darlene told me she was pregnant. I proposed right away." Weston glanced up as Haven set a plate on the table. "Thanks."

She smiled, holding his gaze with a sense of sadness mixed with understanding. No judgment. Just kindness. She was like no one else he'd ever met.

"I'll let you boys get back to your chat. You all look super serious."

Weston took a bite out of the sandwich while he collected his thoughts. "Everyone thought we were too young, and they were right, but all I wanted was a family to call my own. Darlene wanted that too, which is why I don't understand her actions. Even after she was caught, she still wanted me, not Ted." Weston rubbed his temples. "None of it makes sense. She'd been having an affair with Ted for months, but I was deployed so much I had no idea. She went into early labor while I was gone. I missed the birth. I was given special dispensation to leave my post and return stateside to be with my child. When I got there, Alexandra was sick and needed a blood transfusion, but I wasn't a match. That's when I found out I wasn't her father."

"You don't have to have the same blood type as your kid," Ethan said.

"Nope. You don't. But both Darlene and I are A positive. It would be incredibly rare for us to produce a child who is B positive. Ted is B positive." Weston dropped his head back and stared at the ceiling. "I couldn't believe Darlene would do that to me. To us. But for a few days, as I researched how it might be possible, I continued to believe, to hope and pray, that Alexandra was mine. I mean, I'd fallen in love with that little girl. I didn't lose my shit until I learned Ted was a match. I confronted him and Darlene. She denied the affair. She told me that I was being jealous and stupid just because Ted helped our daughter get better. Darlene was adamant I was Alexandra's father, even though all the doctors had told us it was close to impossible, but she hung on to that less than one percent chance."

"Jesus, that had to have been rough," Ethan said. "I'm sorry, man."

"The worst part was she didn't want to do a paternity test. She kept denying the affair, which had to suck for Ted because it was obvious to me that he loved her and knew Alexandra was his kid. I don't know why she wanted to hold on to me."

"She obviously caved in to a paternity test or this birth certificate wouldn't have Ted's name on it. Why?" Ethan asked.

"I called a lawyer. It's one of the things that saved my ass when I pleaded out the criminal charges. The lawyer's the one who helped set up a meeting with the judge and worked to keep it inside the military and not take it to court anywhere else. I didn't have to go to trial. It was all done in a hearing where I pleaded guilty to exactly what I did and nothing more." Weston turned his head and Haven walked by.

She waved and smiled. It conveyed a real sense of warmth and caring and he wasn't used to that from women. Or from anyone. Everyone in his life he kept at arm's length, so no one got close enough to penetrate his tough exterior with that kind of gesture. Perhaps opening up one of the worst emotional wounds of his life with two men he wanted desperately to have the respect of left him wide open to that kind of genuineness.

Whatever it was, he welcomed it.

He winked. The second he did it, he wished he could take it back. It was a knee-jerk reaction to a woman he found incredibly attractive. Both inside and out. Her looks were only part of what drew him to Haven. She was smart and had a wicked sense of humor. Last night, he'd done his best to keep his distance. He'd meant it when he told his cousins he had no desire for lady entanglements. It had been six months since he'd been involved in a relationship and that hadn't ended well. Not because he was the same womanizing asshole he used to be, but because no matter how hard he tried, he couldn't trust.

Rocky kicked him under the table. "What the

fuck was that? I thought you said you were just friends. Friends don't wink."

Weston raked a hand across the top of his head. "I didn't mean anything by it, I swear. Old habits die hard."

"I'll kick your ass if you lay a hand on her," Ethan said with way too much venom laced in every word. "Please continue with your story. You were about to tell us why you beat the crap out of Ted."

Weston cleared his throat. "After the paternity test came back and I learned the disgusting truth that changed my world, I went to a very dark place. I spent a good week drunk. I don't remember shit. I barely remember the altercation with Ted."

"Police reports state you beat him something good," Rocky said.

"I put him in the hospital." Shame filled Weston's heart. His mind flew back to that night. Visions of his fist landing on Ted's face made him cringe. Weston wasn't that man. He hated himself for his actions. Regardless of Ted's betrayal or his hurtful words, he didn't deserve to have his face bashed in. "I'm not proud of what happened. I was arrested and I could have faced the same discharge I ended up with."

"You got off with a slap on the wrist," Rocky said. "How'd that happen?"

"There were witnesses to the fight." Weston let out a long breath.

"What's that supposed to mean?" Ethan asked.

"To this day I struggle to remember and I told the judge that. However, there were people in that bar who came to my defense, stating that Ted was in my face. Poking his finger in the center of my chest. Calling me names. Telling me I wasn't a man and if I had been, Darlene wouldn't have turned to him. Someone told the cops that he shoved me against the wall and at first I did nothing until he spit on me and disparaged my uniform. That's when I went nuts." Weston reached for his water and chugged. "When I woke up in military lockup, I figured my life was over. I'd lost my fiancée. A child that wasn't mine to lose. And now possibly my career and I was only twenty-two." Weston laughed. "I got lucky the judge wanted to hear my side, from me, in his chambers. We had a nice long chat and I poured out my soul. He allowed me to make it right, but that meant I had to leave town."

Ethan cocked his head. "I'm not following two things. The first is how you ended up in a military lockup when local cops arrested you. And the second is, why were you leaving town?"

"There was an MP (military police) at the bar. He was one of the witnesses and talked the cop into letting him handle me," Weston said. "To the second point, the judge thought it best if I had some hard-core training to put my head on straight. He suggested sniper school. Ranger school. All the schools. Of course, after I served my sentence, which was a boatload of community service."

"We always wondered how you managed all that," Rocky said.

"It hung on me, keeping my nose clean. One blemish on my record and that judge would yank me from whatever school or training program and toss me behind bars, throwing the full weight of what could have been my conviction." Weston snapped his fingers. "That judge scared me more than the likes of the two of you."

Ethan laughed, but his expression quickly turned serious. "You got lucky someone believed in you. Have you spoken to him since your discharge?"

Weston nodded. "I felt I owed it to him after everything he did for me and much to my surprise, he is still standing by me. He's been in contact with Fenmore, absolutely mortified that what happened in his chambers made its way to my discharge hearing without his knowledge. He stated he would have loved to testify in front of the review board on my behalf."

"We're glad he gave you a second chance." Rocky held his gaze. "I'm sorry we judged you so harshly without hearing your side of the story." He held up his hand. "I don't condone beating the shit out of a man who didn't toss the first punch, but he certainly egged you on."

"While Ted is an asshole for his part in what he and Darlene did, he didn't deserve to have me beat the crap out of him. I was wrong." Weston swallowed the thick emotion sitting in his throat like hard candy. "But things with us? We're family and all that shit is in the past. Water under the bridge. I'm tired of being angry at everyone. I want my family back and will do whatever it takes to make that happen."

Haven scurried past again, her smile as big as the sun. She made him believe he could do anything. Be anything.

"We want that too, but she's still off-limits," Ethan said with a narrowed stare.

Weston scoffed, shaking his head. "And if Haven wasn't being stalked?"

"Still wouldn't want you near her." Rocky arched a brow. "No offense, but you've left a string of broken hearts a mile long. Maybe it was in reaction to what happened, and that doesn't necessarily make you a bad person. It just makes you not the right person for Haven."

"I stopped being a dick when it comes to women at twenty-seven. Since then, I'm simply and utterly terrified and don't trust members of the opposite sex. They're all liars and that comes from more than one experience." Weston shrugged. While he didn't for one second believe that Haven was anything like a few women he'd dated over the years, the fact she was keeping key information from the people who cared for her most gave him enough reason to pause. "I think she's beautiful and sweet, but all I'm doing is being kind, since I'm the one who's spending twenty-four seven with her. She needs to trust me completely. She won't do that if I'm being stand-offish and aloof."

"You don't have to flirt." Rocky pushed from the booth, glancing at his cell. "Bradly and his little friend are having dinner down the street. That's our cue to go check out the hotel."

"Be careful. I don't believe for one second he and Zelda are sitting around waiting for Haven to do what they want. I wouldn't be surprised if they had backup." Weston rose.

"Zeke is coming with us, so make sure you are on high alert." Rocky knocked his fingers on the table.

"I won't let anything happen to Haven." He smiled as she approached.

"I heard my name and now I'm curious as to why you boys are chatting about me." She stood between Weston and Rocky, leaning closer to Weston.

He had half a mind to step one foot in the opposite direction. Instead, he squeezed her biceps.

That gesture didn't go unnoticed.

"Full disclosure, we're headed to Bradly's hotel while Zeke keeps an eye on him at the restaurant down the street," Ethan said. "It's not horribly busy tonight, and Weston can stay behind the bar. But we'll know if Bradly is on the move. If anything strange happens, you know how to reach us."

Weston rested his hand on the small of Haven's back while he watched his cousins leave On the Rocks bar. While it felt good to have cleared the air with Rocky and Ethan, it would take time for them to become close. To be a real family again. But Weston believed it would happen.

CHAPTER FIVE

Haven leaned against the sink and pressed her hand against her stomach. She closed her eyes and sucked in a deep breath. Deep down, she knew she'd made the right decision. Not only was she ill-prepared to be a mother, but having Bradly's baby would have been the ultimate nightmare.

When she strolled by Weston's table and heard the conversation, her heart ripped from her chest.

The door opened, and Weston waltzed into the kitchen.

She swiped at her cheeks.

"Hey." Weston raced to her side. He ran his hands up and down her arms. "What's wrong? Did you hear from Bradly?"

"No." She inhaled sharply, letting it out in a

swoosh. "But when he comes around, sometimes it gets overwhelming. He plays games, and I try to figure out what he will do next, which is impossible. Like why is he choosing to stay in town? Why did he bring Zelda?"

"He's trying to rattle all of us to push us off our game." Weston lifted her chin with his thumb and forefinger. "I need to get back out there. You take all the time you need back here. I can cover your tables and the bar for as long as you need."

"I won't be long. I promise."

"Don't worry about it." He palmed her face, rubbing his thumb across her cheek. He inched closer. His hot breath tickled her skin.

She swallowed.

His soft lips pressed against her mouth. It was a tender, sweet kiss. Not overtly romantic, but it sent shock waves across her body.

She flattened her hand on the center of his chest. His heart pounded against her fingers. She could barely tell where one beat stopped and the next one started.

He took a step back. "Sorry. I meant to kiss your cheek."

"Right," she whispered.

"I'll see you in the main room whenever you're ready." He turned on his heel and disappeared.

She pressed her fingers to her lips. Wow. That had been quite the kiss. Her entire body still tingled with delight. A sensation she hadn't felt in years.

Sex had become a non-experience. Anytime she was required to perform the act, she managed to escape into the deepest recesses of her mind and go somewhere peaceful. A meadow filled with flowers where she could lie under the warm sun. Or a raging river where she would paddle with feverish intent to get to the end of the rapids.

Anything to escape the reality of what she'd allowed herself to become.

A whore.

She couldn't even say she was a sex worker because she didn't get to keep the money. Sure, she drove an expensive car, wore designer clothes, and appeared to have it all.

But that was an illusion. She literally had nothing.

She adjusted her apron. Ethan, Zeke, and Rocky were keeping an eye on Bradly and Zelda. Weston would take care of her if anyone dared showed their face in the bar. She had nothing to worry about.

Except that damn book.

There was a part of her that wondered if she hadn't taken it, would Bradly be threatening her all the time? Deep down, she knew the answer because she saw what happened to Kate.

Poor Kate.

Bradly had sworn to Haven that Kate wouldn't be harmed. That she could leave without any consequences. Two months later, Kate was found in a hotel, dead.

An overdose.

Haven didn't believe it was accidental or intentional. Bradly had her killed, plain and simple, but she couldn't prove it. Three weeks later, Haven snuck out in the middle of the night and made her way back to Fallport. She thought her parents would welcome her back with open arms.

She was sadly mistaken.

They tossed her out on her ass. They didn't care about what happened, only about the mistakes she'd made and how those made them look.

She squared her shoulders and pushed open the doors that led into the main bar. She needed to push all that out of her mind and focus on the current problem.

How to get Bradly out of her life for good.

She thought it hinged on keeping the book

hidden from everyone. She questioned that decision. Perhaps Weston would know what to do.

"I've closed out two tables for you." Weston set three drinks on a tray. "These belong to those ladies over there." He pointed.

She glanced over her shoulder. Her heart lurched in her throat. She didn't know what was worse. Dealing with Zelda or having to face people she once called friends. "Thanks." She lifted the tray and made her toward Emily, Sydney, and Pamela. At one time, they were best friends. They did everything together. Told each other their deepest secrets. Shared their wildest dreams

But now, the trio wouldn't give her the time of day.

"Here you go, ladies. One lemon drop, an apple martini, and a chocolate espresso martini." She set the drinks down in front of the trio. They'd been in enough for her to know who ordered what. "Would you like to order any food this evening?"

"Is the new bartender on the menu?" Pamela asked. "He's yummy."

"I hope someone warned him about you," Sydney said. "I'd hate for him to think he stood a chance with you, only to learn he has to pay for it."

"I'll be sure to let him know ahead of time," Haven mumbled. "Now, can I take your order?"

"We're going to have the appetizer platter." Emily handed the menus to Haven.

"Coming right up." Haven made her rounds to the rest of her tables, making sure everyone had what they needed and clearing any dirty dishes before slipping behind the bar.

"Everything okay?" Weston tossed a rag over his shoulder. "You have a crinkle in your forehead and you're sporting a frown. Outside of when Bradly showed his ugly face, I'm used to you smiling."

She dumped all the dirty glasses and plates in the appropriate bins. "Sometimes it's a lot being back in Fallport."

"Isn't it your hometown? I would think you have a lot of friends."

"Not anymore." She laughed. "Except your cousins, Zeke, and most of the crew at search and rescue. Otherwise, everyone in Fallport thinks of me as a leper."

Weston tucked a few stray pieces of hair behind her ear. "I take it you're referring to the three girls sitting at the front table."

"They were my closest friends in high school. We did everything together. Even went to the same college. As freshman, we roomed in a quad together, but they joined a sorority."

"You didn't want to?"

"God, no. They wanted to be popular. In with a certain crowd. I wanted to do well in school. Get good grades. But I also only had a partial scholarship and had to pay for a large portion of my education. I had to work. They didn't. Things got weird with us, and then I made some pretty poor choices and we haven't been friends since." She lifted one of the trays. "I'm sorry. I was already in a sour mood before those three showed up and they tend to make it all worse. I don't mean to dump it all on you."

"You're not." He pointed to the tray. "Would you like me to take those to the back, or would you like a break from all the people?"

"You can do it. I'm used to the stares and snide remarks."

He squeezed her shoulder. "I'll be right back."

No sooner did he disappear into the kitchen than Pamela set her drink on the counter and leaned against the bar. "Where did the bartender go?"

"Is something wrong with your drink?" Haven asked.

Pamela pursed her lips. "No. I just wanted to ask him a question about it."

Wonderful. It didn't take a genius to know that Pamela either wanted to warn Weston about Haven's sordid past, or even worse, flirt with the man because Pamela was always on the hunt. She had a taste for new blood and lately, she went after every new search and rescue man that Ethan brought to Fallport. Before Haven could answer, Weston strolled through the doors.

"I have tables to check on." She squeezed Weston's biceps. "Holler if you need me." And he just might.

WESTON STARED at Haven's backside as she strolled away. Great. Left alone with a woman who obviously wanted to use him to butter her toast in the morning.

The young woman climbed up on a stool. She waved. "Hi. I'm Pamela." She pointed to her drink. "You make the best lemon drop I've ever had."

"Thank you," Weston said. "I'm glad you like it."

"You're new here." Pamela smiled.

"I am." Weston didn't want to be rude, but he also didn't want to spend his time chatting with this vixen. He knew the type well, and he wanted nothing to do with a woman who was searching for a specific man to put a ring on her finger and that's precisely what Pamela was looking for. He didn't need to have a conversation to figure that out.

"And are you going to tell me your name?"

"It's Weston."

"Well, Weston. How do you like our little town so far?" She leaned forward, pressing her arms against the sides of her chest, enhancing her cleavage.

Six years ago that trick might have gotten his attention. He would have even been able to ignore the fake personality so he could spend a little time in a woman's arms. But not anymore. He'd learned that when a lady had *that* look in her eyes, run and run fast. They weren't worth the trouble.

"I haven't seen much of it yet, but I'm enjoying it." He refreshed a beer for the gentleman at the corner.

"Well, you're in luck because I was born and raised here. I know all the best places. The things you should do and what to avoid. Growing up, I used to give tour guides." She batted her lashes. "I know things about this town that even the mayor doesn't."

"Fallport has guided tours?"

"My parents own a rather large piece of property about ten miles outside of town. It's been in my family for generations. Before the Civil War, it was one of the largest plantations in the South. It became a battleground between the North and South during the war."

"And which side did your family stand on?" This could be an interesting answer.

"If you're asking if the plantation owned slaves, of course they did. Most people back then did." She held up her finger. "But my family never liked the word slaves and they treated those who worked for them with respect. They gave them skills and an education and were for freedom. They wanted to end slavery and worked with the North to help make that happen. We're in the history books. I could show you."

Weston didn't believe one word that came out of Pamela's mouth. It was her way of rewriting history to make herself feel better for her own privilege. The right thing to do, in Weston's mind, would be to own the injustice. Apologize for it. Teach what really happened and make sure history never repeated itself. But that was impossible with the Pamelas of the world. They wanted everyone to believe they were always in the right.

But if that were the case, there would have never been a civil war in the first place. It happened. His father's side of the family had come from the South. They had all owned slaves. They weren't proud of their history, but they didn't try to shoehorn it into something it wasn't.

"I'll take your word for it." He pointed to her drink. "Shall I make you another one?"

"Not just yet." She ran her finger over the rim of the glass. "So, I take it you were in the military."

He nodded.

"What branch?"

"Army." He knew he needed to be nice, but the last thing he wanted to do was engage in small talk with this chick.

"May I ask why you left?"

"It was time." Weston shifted his gaze, hoping Haven might come and rescue him from flirty pants, but Haven was currently occupied taking a table's order.

Pamela glanced over her shoulder. "Let me give you a piece of unsolicited advice."

This should be good. "What's that?"

"I realize you have to work with Haven, but if I were you, I'd stay away from her outside of this place."

"Why's that?" Weston asked.

Pamela wiggled her index finger, motioning for

him to come closer. "I'm surprised no one has told you about her past yet."

"Everyone has one." He rested his elbows on the bar.

"Hers is a little more colorful," Pamela whispered. "And she can pretend she's changed, but we all know she hasn't."

"What's that supposed to mean?"

Pamela leaned over the bar. "In college, she worked at an escort agency." Pamela lowered her chin and put on a pouty face. "Or so she said that's all it was, but she recruited a girl I knew who told me one of the requirements was to sleep with the clients. Haven might not work for the agency anymore, but she's still having sex for money."

Weston shouldn't be entertaining this conversation, but he found himself wanting answers to questions that had formed long before Pamela put ideas in his head. "And you know this how?"

"This is a small town and people talk."

"So, it's hearsay." Weston pressed his hands on the counter and stood tall. "No offense, but I don't listen to idle gossip."

"It's not. It's fact. Ask anyone. They'll tell you the same thing I just did." Pamela stiffened her spine. Her face hardened.

"I'm curious, why did you feel the need to share that with me?" He knew the answer, but he wanted to hear Pamela's version of her truth. Weston could learn a lot about Pamela and perhaps gain a little insight into Haven that way. It wasn't that he believed what Pamela had said, at least not in the way Pamela had presented it, but it helped him understand why Haven chose not to tell him anything.

"Haven would like people—especially those new to town—to believe she's a victim. That she didn't do anything wrong. But she did. She does. A zebra doesn't change their stripes, if you know what I mean." Pamela lifted her drink. "I was just trying to look out for you so that you didn't fall into her trap, because that's what she does. She gets you to trust her, and then before you know it, you're under her spell. Kind of like the owner of this bar and a couple of his buddies. I wouldn't be surprised if they were clients."

"Are you suggesting that Zeke pays her for sex?" Weston wanted to laugh out loud. That had to be the most ludicrous thing he'd ever heard. "And are you tossing Rocky and Ethan into that as well?"

"They are always defending her." Pamela

shrugged. "Always around her. It makes the most sense."

"I'd be careful about spreading rumors. You're making dangerous assumptions about people, especially three men who—from what I have seen—are dedicated to their families."

"You haven't been in town long enough to know these people like I do. I'm just trying to look out for the new guy in town." She flashed a smile and batted her eyes. "I'd be happy to show you around."

"I appreciate that, but I believe I have that covered. I failed to mention that I have two cousins who live in Fallport." He did his best to keep from smiling when she jerked her head back and her nose crinkled.

"Cousins?"

"Yeah. Rocky and Ethan." He took the towel and wiped down the counter. "My turn to dish out a little advice. Stop talking about people behind their backs. You're working on half-truths and downright lies."

"Actually, I'm not." She lifted her drink to her lips and gulped. "Why don't you ask her about what she did for a living for the past five years and find out for yourself." Pamela jumped from the stool. Her heels clicked against the wood floor as her hips swayed while she strolled across the bar with her head held high in the proverbial sky.

Haven carried a tray of empty plates behind the bar. She sorted the dirties into the appropriate bins. "You two looked chummy."

"There's only been one woman in my life that I've ever really called a bitch." Weston chuckled. "She will make two."

"She's not my favorite person either." Haven leaned against the counter. "I'm a little afraid to ask what happened during the conversation."

"It's not a discussion we should have here." He had no idea how to approach Haven with the intel Pamela had dumped in his lap. He could call his cousins or even Zeke for clarification, but he'd prefer to hear about Haven's life from the source.

Part of him wondered if she'd tell him the truth. If it were him, he wasn't sure he would. He understood better than most the shame and regret that came with huge mistakes and how they followed you no matter where you went in the world.

CHAPTER SIX

The only thing Haven wanted to do was wash the grime off her face, put on her favorite pajamas, climb between the sheets, and cuddle with her dog.

However, Weston had made it clear he wanted to chat, and she knew it had to do with his conversation with Pamela. Haven had a good idea what that had entailed. She should have never begged Zeke and his friends to keep her secret from Weston. While everyone who worked at the bar knew how much she wanted to put her past in the rearview, that wouldn't prevent other people in town from airing her dirty laundry.

And putting their own spin on it.

She lifted the shade in her bedroom. Gunner sniffed around in the backyard, looking for the best spot to do his business while Weston pressed his cell to his ear. He probably called one of his cousins or Zeke for clarification on whatever story Pamela had seen fit to spew from her ugly mouth.

Haven turned and pressed her fingers to her lips. Weston's kiss only lasted a few seconds, but it had rocked her world unexpectedly. No man had ever treated her with such kindness and respect while engaging in something so intimate. Perhaps that was because she made sure physical contact wasn't personal. When she'd first started at the escort agency, all she had to endure were a few inappropriate comments, a couple of pats on the ass, and maybe a disgusting kiss or two by a dirty old man. That was it.

Until she met Bradly. He swept her off her feet. He took her to fancy restaurants. Showered her with expensive gifts. He made her feel like the sun rose and set on only her and no one else. He told her he didn't want to be her client. That he wanted more. A relationship. He said he had fallen in love and he would do whatever it took to make her happy.

Within two months of her moving into his home, she realized she'd signed her life over to the devil, but it was too late. She had no money of her own. Bradly controlled her every move. She was trapped.

Quickly, she shed her work clothes and put on sweats and a T-shirt before making her way to the kitchen. She found a bottle of red wine and poured herself a large glass. She needed to calm her nerves. Drinking wasn't necessarily the smartest move, but taking the edge off before facing Weston and his questions had become a moral imperative.

The door opened, and Gunner went right for his spot on the end of the sofa. She opted to join her dog. Unfortunately, Weston helped himself to what was left in the bottle of wine and joined them, making himself way too comfortable by kicking off his shoes and placing his bare feet on the coffee table.

"This isn't bad." He clanked his glass against hers and smiled.

"Zeke lets me take a bottle now and then from the bar. That's the house blend." She scratched Gunner's head. "What did he have to say about Bradly?"

"Bradly and Zelda had dinner and then went back to the hotel. They were watching us watch them, according to Zeke. Right now, it's a pissing contest." Weston set his glass down. "Brayden found out that Bradly's been looking into expanding his business to Fallport. He has a meeting tomorrow with a real estate agent about purchasing an office building in the next town over. We're trying to figure out if this is a bona fide option for him, or if he's trying to scare you."

"His businesses are bullshit," she mumbled.

"I spent a little time behind the bar tonight reading up on his legit business side." Weston rested his arm on the backside of the couch. "I hate to admit it, but the man's impressive."

"He launders money through businesses he invests in after promising the world to the owners he damn near puts out of business. It's all very *Ozark* or *Breaking Bad,* if you watch those kinds of shows."

"Two of my favorites. But how do you know about the laundering? Is this something you've seen firsthand?" Weston shifted. He lifted her glass, setting it aside. "My cousins didn't have much time to talk. So please, help me understand about Bradly so I can better protect you."

"Are you asking because of the information you got from them or because of the conversation you had with Pamela?"

"Both," he said.

Her eyes burned with hot tears. This shouldn't be so hard anymore. What difference did it make if Weston knew the truth? Even if he remained in Fallport forever, it wasn't as if he would stay in her life long term.

Weston palmed her cheek. "I'm the last person to judge someone else."

"I'm sure what Pamela told you isn't far from the truth." She pushed his hand away.

He cocked his head. "I'm positive it is; otherwise, you're selling your body to my cousins."

She leaned over and hugged her dog. He whimpered, licking her face as if to give her moral support. "Okay, that part isn't true." She snagged her glass and stood, putting distance between her and Weston. His kindness was too much and honestly, she didn't trust it. Other men had shown her compassion, only to expect a discount on services for their efforts. She wanted to believe he was different. That he was like his cousins. Like Zeke, Brayden, and the rest of the search and rescue team. Weston had all the same qualities. He had the same mannerisms as Rocky and he looked similar to Ethan. She found it hard to believe that he could have ever hurt another human. His soul was too deep and full of compassion.

But he was still a man and she no longer had faith in her ability to read people's true intentions.

"We all do dumb things in our youth. We trust

the wrong people. Get taken advantage of. It happens to the best of us."

"This goes beyond being young and stupid." She downed three good gulps. "In the beginning, I knew what I was doing." Haven had to believe Weston was one of the good guys. At the very least, someone who would at least keep his judgmental thoughts to himself. Regardless, she needed to be the one to tell her story.

"The escort agency," he stated as if he knew her entire fucking life story.

She laughed. "Yeah, that." She leaned against the mantel, taking another slow sip. "It started out innocent enough. I mean, I had my doubts and was ready to run at the first sign of something wonky, but when you get paid a thousand dollars for one night of doing nothing but looking pretty in a short dress, high heels, and not much of anything else, you're willing to give it a second try. And then a third. A fourth. And so on. For six months I went on dates at least four nights a week. Sometimes more. I was only propositioned once and that man never returned. It was easy money and I was rolling in it. Not only could I pay my bills, but come the end of my first year, I got an apartment. I didn't have to live on campus, which was amazing. My parents were pissed but got over it when I told them I was doing an internship. Things were great."

"And then you met Bradly," Weston said with an edge to his voice. One that was impossible to ignore. "I take it he started as a client."

She nodded. "For months he showered me with gifts. He wined and dined me. It was a good gig, but he wanted more and at first I wouldn't give it to him."

"I don't mean to sound crass, but eventually you did."

"It wasn't like that. Believe it or not, he never paid me for sex. But he did want us to be a couple. Or at least that's what I thought. He would get super jealous when I went out with other clients, even though I swore to him that nothing was going on. But he would ask me questions about how it all worked and who the other girls were. He wanted to know how they were recruited." She tugged at her ponytail, releasing her long hair. "Next thing I knew, he bought the agency. I thought it was some grandiose gesture, but it turned out to be the beginning of my nightmare."

"How so?"

"Jesus, you're really going to make me tell this story in great detail, aren't you?"

"I don't need the nitty-gritty, but it will help me better understand what he wants."

She blinked out a couple of tears. They burned a path down her face. "The agency was legit before he purchased it. There was no sex involved. None. And if there ever was, the girls got fired and the clients were blackballed. Bradly saw this as an opportunity to exploit and control another passion of his that I didn't know existed. You see, he was using me for information. He wanted that agency from the very beginning and I was his ticket."

"I understand this is difficult for you, but you're beating around the bush."

She eased into the chair across from him and rubbed her hands up and down her knees. "Bradly uses the girls in the agency to blackmail some pretty powerful people. He'll video the exchange of money, the discussion of sexual favors, and then the act itself."

"Is that how he controlled you?"

"Yes and no," she admitted. "He first got me to believe I was in love with him. That we were this great couple. But that changed after he had the agency. By then, he'd gotten me addicted to pills. I had dropped out of college and helped him recruit other girls like me. He would threaten to tell my parents and when that no longer mattered, he'd tell me he would send them videos of me…" She let out a long breath. "I'm shocked he hasn't uploaded them somewhere or followed through with that one. But even that I don't care about. My parents have disowned me, so it doesn't matter."

"Oh, babe, yes, it does. I understand shame. Self-hatred. I know what it's like to be the black sheep and to have everyone in your family look at you like you've done this big horrible thing that's totally unforgivable. It's hard when they only look at one part and not all the pieces that led to the end result."

"When I stopped caring what he did to me, he would start hurting the new girls in front of me. Five weeks ago, I was prepared to go back when he sent me a picture of a twenty-one-year-old with her face bashed in. Rocky got in the way of that. There is a part of me that wishes he hadn't because while Bradly has never killed anyone himself, I know he's hired people to do it. It's a struggle to keep myself safe, knowing he could hurt someone else while trying to control me."

"But you can't let him kill you either." Weston pinched the bridge of his nose. "You're a victim in all this."

"Am I, though? Because in many ways I was complicit."

"Did he hit you?"

"Of course he did," she whispered.

"Then you're a victim. No other way to look at it, so stop beating yourself up for being young and naive," Weston said. "What is it that you took from him? Why is he coming back here? I need you to tell me so we can put an end to this once and for all."

"He wants me back."

"No. He's done with you. He has Zelda to fill your shoes." Weston stood and inched closer. Getting down on his knees, he took her hands. "You have something that he sees as valuable. That's what he wants and once he gets it, I shudder to think what he'll do with you. That said, he'll do whatever it takes to get it back."

She jerked her head. "He'll kill me if I hand it over to the police." She covered her mouth.

"I'm not the cops. Whatever it is that you took, it's not going to keep you alive forever." He took her chin in his palm. "My cousins will serve my head on a platter, but I promise I won't tell them what it is."

"You'd do that?"

"For now. But eventually, we'll have to fill them in after I make sense of whatever it is."

"The problem is the book doesn't really prove anything. It's just the names of some powerful people. Men he's hooked up with some of the girls who work for him. However, that by itself isn't criminal."

"I suppose it's not. Is there anything else?" Weston asked.

"He's also got a few ladies who are daughters of some very rich families who have ended up employed at the agency. Their names are in the book. There's also a section of locations. In the back of the book there are dates and next to those are random numbers and letters. But I don't know what some of it means."

"Sounds like he's using a code. That can be cracked and we can go to the police then."

"I don't think that's a good idea." She shook her head. "Even if we did give this to the cops, it would be my word against his and he does have me on video. He'll use that to discredit the whore who took money for sex and I won't be able to deny it." That wasn't the only reason she didn't want to give it to the police.

"Hey. You're not a whore."

"I was."

He squeezed her chin. "I don't ever want to hear

you call yourself that again. I've killed people; does that make me a murderer?"

"Excuse me?"

"While deployed on missions, I've been in situations where it was kill or be killed. I had to make the difficult decision to take a life in a split second and I sometimes still have nightmares about it."

"You can't compare what you did defending this country to what I did." She batted his hand away and abruptly stood.

"It might not be the best comparison." He rose, taking her into his arms. "But in some ways, you weren't given a choice." He pressed his finger over her lips. "Did you sleep with him for money when it first started?"

"I never slept with Bradly for money. At least not in that way. But after things changed, he sent me out. He told me to go out there and do what I did to…" She swallowed a guttural groan.

He kissed her temple. "Bradly is a monster. He manipulated you." He arched a brow. "Tell me this. When did you start taking any kind of drugs?"

"A few months after I started going out on dates with him. He felt bad because my studies were suffering from all the nights he employed my company."

"Where no sex was involved, right?"

She nodded. "He told me the pills would help me focus, and they did. But then our relationship changed and he bought the agency." She let out a long breath. "He asked me if I wanted to run it for him. The income was more than I could have imagined. It seemed like a great opportunity, so I dropped out of college." She laughed. "Looking back, I can see all the danger signs."

"That's because hindsight is perfect vision." He pressed his warm, soft lips over her mouth.

She wanted to pull away, but instead, gripped his shoulder, allowing the kiss to linger, enjoying the comfort his embrace offered. Outside of a couple of boys she dated in high school, Bradly had been her only relationship and that hadn't been a healthy one. In reality, she had been his property. A woman he controlled through fear, sex, and money. The safety she thought Bradly had provided had been an illusion. A trap. It had all been a way to draw her close so he could control her every move.

It left her with no ability to discern if what she was feeling in the arms of Weston was real or not. She wanted so desperately to believe there were good men. She knew that Zeke and his friends were as true as they came, but they were different. They didn't want anything. They had wives and children. They didn't view her as a product. As something that could be purchased. She didn't know Weston. He could be like everyone else. Or worse. He could honestly think he could see beyond her past.

He palmed her cheek. "You can see where you screwed up. That's half the battle."

Resting her head on his chest, she caved to his kindness. "I wish I felt that way. The majority of the people in this town see me as a vulture. A predator. They tell their children to stay away. Women look at me like I'm going to try to seduce husbands or teenage sons. They worry I'll turn the young women here into sex workers. And the men." She took a step back, shaking her head. "They are offering me money, asking if it's enough for specific sexual acts."

"Right after I put my ex's husband in the hospital, people would walk on the other side of the street. My family wouldn't talk to me. But the worst was when someone asked if I would be willing to beat someone up for them."

"That's terrible." She flopped back into the chair. "But it's not the same."

"I didn't say it was. But people do have the ability to forget."

"Not in this town they don't."

"It's only been two months." He lifted her wine and handed it to her. "And Bradly showing up isn't helping. We need to find a way to end this, and I believe it starts with that book," he said. "I'd like to see it."

Rage crept into her toes. It inched up to her ankles and spread like a wildfire through the rest of her body, engulfing her like flames. "All this sweet talk. The kindness. The tender kisses. It was all just to get to the fucking book." Slowly, she forced herself out of the chair. Her breath came hard and deep. She stared into his intense dark eyes. "Zeke and your cousins put you here because you're good with the ladies. They figured because they couldn't get me to even tell them I took something, maybe you could kiss it out of me." She set her glass down; otherwise, she was going to toss it in his face. "You used my vulnerability and—"

"That's not what's going on here," Weston said with a narrowed stare. "While I shouldn't have kissed you at all, I don't regret it. I'm attracted to you, a fact I can't deny." He raised his hands, showing his palms. "I'm honestly trying to help you."

"Why? Why do you care? I'm no one to you."

"After Darlene and I broke up, I spent years rebuilding my life and I'm damn proud of what I accomplished. Sniper school. Ranger school. Those are not easy things. I built a great career and I had no one to share it with. Not a soul. Part of that was my fault. I let my family believe a lot of things about me. I chose not to correct them. I came to Fallport to make amends to my cousins and hopefully repair all my family relationships."

"What the hell are you talking about?"

"Protecting you started out as a very selfish act. It was all about mending my own family." He lowered his chin. "In some ways, it's still about proving to them I'm not the same dumbass kid they remember. But the more time I spend with you, the more I like you. That might be dangerous because I find myself constantly wanting to kiss you."

"Even after all that I've told you? Everything that I've done?" She wanted to believe his words—his actions—but her past dictated she couldn't. She studied his unwavering expression. His soulful eyes spoke to her heart. There was no judgment. No disdain. But that didn't make it any easier for her to trust that he wouldn't walk out of her life when things got tough.

"We all have a past. I put a man in the hospital with my bare hands. I broke his nose, four fingers, his arm, and three ribs. I managed to puncture a lung and he had to stay in the hospital for twelve days, two of them on a ventilator."

She took a step back. "I overheard your conversation about your ex-girlfriend. What she did regarding the baby and what you did, but I didn't realize it was that bad."

"I was a jerk and I will regret that moment for the rest of my life."

"How did you get a reputation for being a ladies' man?" If she expected Weston to ignore what she'd done, she needed to give him the same respect. But in order to do that, she needed to understand more of his past.

"Same way every other guy does. I dated a lot of women and didn't have relationships." He strolled toward the kitchen and leaned against the counter. "I didn't trust women, but I liked having them in my arms." He shrugged. "I tried to date girls who didn't want a ring or a long-term thing, but a few managed to sneak past my radar. Unfortunately, I broke a few hearts. Again, something I'm not proud of."

"When did you stop being a womanizer?"

"God, I hate that word." He leaned against the counter. "And I wouldn't describe myself that way. To me, a womanizer is someone who disrespects a lady. Someone who has no regard for her as a person. I was never like that. I just dated a lot and didn't want to be in a committed relationship." He held up his hand. "To answer your question, I settled down a little in my late twenties."

"And now? Do you have long-term relationships? Do you want to get married someday?"

"I still have major trust issues with women and honestly, I don't know if I'll ever be in the right frame of mind for marriage. Anyone I date, I'm open and honest about these things, especially that I'm not sure I could commit long term."

She rinsed out her glass and set it next to sink. "But you wanted it once. And you were open to a family."

"I was twenty-one when Darlene got pregnant. I was a stupid kid. I had no idea what I really wanted. At thirty-five the only thing I'm sure of is that I want to reconcile with my parents and the rest of my family. I've missed them." He held her gaze. "Not that I mind sharing, but why all the questions?"

"Zeke and your cousins asked you to help them protect me from Bradly. I appreciate all that you're doing. But the kissing is confusing me and if I'm going to trust you with my past, I want to know yours, especially because I was told to watch out."

"That's fair." He nodded. "I like you and if I'm

being totally honest, being more than friends is quite appealing. I think you're intelligent, kind, sweet, and sexy as hell. I'm no longer doing this solely because it benefits me and helps me get into the good graces of my cousins. I genuinely care about you and want to make sure that Bradly is not only out of your life, but that he gets what he deserves." He ran a hand over his growing beard. "I'm confused as well. I've been warned numerous times to keep my distance. That I have one job when it comes to you and that my cousins and Zeke will most likely fire me and run me out of town if I continue flirting with you, and yet I can't seem to stop myself."

"Thank you." She strolled around the other side of the counter. Physical contact with men didn't come easily anymore. Even an innocent hug could make her tense up. But not once did Weston's touch make her feel as though she were being violated. Or disrespected in any way. There was an unexplainable instant connection and a deep desire that she'd never experienced before. Not even early on with Bradly when she believed she was falling in love.

She needed to trust that it was real, even if it wouldn't last beyond getting rid of Bradly.

Weston cocked his head. "For what exactly?"

"For being honest on why you're here and how

you feel." Tentatively, she placed her hand over his and let the warmth of his skin ease her fear. "Knowing that there are two parts to it helps me understand whatever this is." She waved her hand between them. "Outside of Zeke and his wife, along with your cousins and their wives, I don't know what a healthy relationship looks like."

"What about your parents?"

"Not the worst marriage, but certainly not a good role model for me." She laughed. "My mom is trapped in an old-fashioned world that forces her to live one way, but tells her she's totally free to do whatever she chooses. It's not true, especially because my parents don't have money." She lifted her finger. "They did raise me to believe I could be whatever I wanted. That all it took was a little hard work. However, they enforced gender roles. I could be a doctor, but a nurse might be more in line with being a wife and mother. I could be lawyer but maybe a clerk or a different career in the legal field that suited having a family."

"Your parents are traditionalists. Nothing necessarily wrong with that for them."

"Nope, but it wasn't for me and I rebelled. Hard."

"Wait a second. But didn't you tell me you were friends with Miss Fancy Pants Pamela? Cheerleader. Snag a rich husband and settle down eventually."

"For the record, it was the dance team and that has nothing to do with my rebellion. Pamela and the rest of my friends all majored in communications. They went there with the idea of maybe meeting someone in pre-law or anyone with ambition who could support a certain way of life. They don't want careers. They want to be taken care of. I didn't want that, but I ended up on the other end of the spectrum."

"What did you want? Or do want," Weston asked.

"Don't laugh, but I wanted to be a cop or maybe an FBI agent."

"Why would I laugh at that?" he said. "If I hadn't been dishonorably discharged, that's exactly where I would have gone. Or maybe DEA. Or some other kind of law enforcement. But that dishonorable part now makes it impossible."

"Not if you get it overturned." She squeezed his hand. "Sorry, I heard that part too."

He laughed. "You're a little eavesdropper, aren't you."

She shrugged. "I thought you all were talking about me, so I wanted to know. I didn't mean to pry into your life."

"It saved me the trouble of having to repeat it."

"Can I ask you a question?"

"Sure."

"Will you go into law enforcement if your discharge is overturned?" she asked.

"I can't allow myself to even think about that right now."

"Why not?"

He glanced toward the ceiling. "I don't want to get my hopes up and have them crushed if things don't work out. You, on the other hand, there's no stopping you from following that dream. I know for a fact that Brayden has connections inside the FBI. And Zeke and my cousins have connections with the local police. It's all possible for you."

"I know. He's made it perfectly clear that he'd be willing to call in a few favors, but I have to finish my degree and get Bradly out of my life for good."

Weston arched a brow. "That brings us full circle to the book."

"It's late. I'm tired. Can we do that tomorrow?"

"Is there any reason I can't look at it tonight?"

"I suppose not. Wait here. I'll be right back." She strolled into her bedroom and pulled open her closet, glancing over her shoulder to make sure Weston hadn't followed. She kept the book in one of her shoeboxes under a pair of boots. It probably wasn't the safest of hiding places but it was better than under her mattress. That seemed so cliché. Clutching it tightly in her fingers, she made her way back to the kitchen. She was putting complete faith in a man she just met and that should frighten her as much, if not more, as being trapped in a never-ending cycle of looking over her shoulder. But it didn't. "I'm not sure any of this will make much sense to you."

"Maybe not, but I still want to read through it."

She shifted her gaze between the sofa and Weston. "I'm sure I'll be okay if you want to sleep in your own apartment. I've got Gunner."

"No. Not when we know Bradly is in town. I'll feel better if I'm in the same space as you."

"Gunner's not going to sleep well knowing you're out here. He'll keep scratching at the door."

"Leave it open. He can come and go as he pleases. He won't bother me. Besides, I'll be up doing a perimeter check every couple of hours and I'd rather him be on high alert while I'm doing that. I'm just sorry if that will disturb you."

"I'll be fine." She leaned in and kissed Weston's cheek. She didn't want to encourage him, but she had to admit, she enjoyed the close proximity of his lips. "Good night, Weston."

"Sleep well, Haven."

That wouldn't happen until Bradly was arrested and put away for a very long time.

CHAPTER SEVEN

"Come on, Gunner." Weston patted the end of the sofa. "I can make room for both of us."

Gunner leaped onto the couch and plopped his body over Weston's legs with a big snort and sigh.

Weston laughed. One of these days, once he was all settled, he would march down to the animal shelter and find himself a dog. However, he suspected he'd never find one as good as Gunner. "I don't have the bandwidth to go through this book, but I should." He flipped through a couple of pages. Names and dates, but it didn't make sense. He would have to make notes so he could try to make connections and that would take time. Not to mention a concentration level that he didn't have at the moment. Unfortunately, his mind wandered to the intriguing woman sleeping in the next room.

Haven was stronger than she gave herself credit for. She'd endured more than most at her age. He understood why she blamed herself for what had happened and respected her even more for taking ownership of the direction of her life. But that didn't change the facts. She was still a victim in whatever game Bradly had been playing. Bradly's thirst for power and control had become her nightmare. He was a narcissist who preyed on those in their darkest hour. He used his charm and position to find blind spots, and then he exploited those traits.

He was a master manipulator and he could do it to the most intelligent people. Bradly was the kind of man who could speak anyone's language. That's what made him so dangerous.

Weston flipped a page and scanned the names.

He bolted to an upright position.

Gunner yelped.

"Sorry." He leaned over and patted the dog's head while staring at one name.

Wicker.

What the fuck was Phil Wicker's name doing in Bradly's book? A million other questions flashed in Weston's brain. But only one logical answer formed.

Wicker had to be a client.

Weston snagged his cell and snapped a photograph of the page. He recognized other names, but he didn't know the men personally. He didn't understand the dates. However, he wanted to go through his own personal timeline. Fairfax, Virginia—where Haven went to college—wasn't far from CIA headquarters. It certainly was plausible that Wicker could have used an escort service. According to Haven, the one she worked for was known for being discreet and had high-powered clients.

That held true considering some of the names in the book were senators, congressmen, and other key figures in DC.

Gunner whined, raising his head.

The sound of feet scurrying across the floor tickled Weston's ears. "Haven?"

She appeared at the side of the sofa, holding her cell in her hand. Tears dribbled down her cheeks. "Bradly's threatening to turn information about me over to the police."

"What kind of information?"

"I don't know exactly. He only states that it won't be good for me. That I could see real prison time if I don't return what is his. I have two days."

Weston made room on the sofa. "May I see the

text?"

"Sure." She handed him her phone as she eased between him and the dog. "I know if I give it to him nothing will change. He'll still come after me. The idea that he wants to set up a business here freaks me out."

"That could be to put pressure on you." Weston scrolled through the texts. "There are some interesting names in that book. How many of them do you know personally?"

She jerked her head. "You want to know who I slept with? As clients?"

Shit. That's not exactly what he meant to imply. "I'm only asking who you've met. Or had contact with."

"Most of them." She leaned back and closed her eyes. "When Bradly took over the agency, I was the one who set up the dates. I was the contact. I vetted the clients and the girls." She let out a long breath. "Half of what's in that book, I put there."

"Excuse me?"

Opening her eyes, she sat up and took the book, flipping it open. "I kept track of the clients and who they were matched with. I kept track of where they met. But this back here." She turned the pages. "He wrote this and I have no idea what it means."

"Are you afraid of turning this over because it implicates you in some wrongdoing?"

She laughed. "Essentially, Bradly turned me into a madam and I allowed him to do it." She shook her head. "I should have seen it coming, but I didn't."

"Explain to me why you believe that."

"When Bradly first bought the agency, it was still legit. But slowly, the girls were expected to sleep with the clients. If they didn't, they were consequences. I didn't want to believe it, but when I questioned Bradly, I was met with my first knuckle sandwich."

Weston palmed her cheek.

She batted his hand away. "I had moved into his house and believed he and I were an item. I had given up everything, and yet silly me believed I was still in control of my own destiny and tried to leave."

"What happened?"

"I was pulled over five miles from the house for a bogus drunk driving charge. He told me he could get it dropped if I did the right thing and came home. After that, any time I dared to question him, he would either hurt me or one of the girls. That's when he started sending me out on *special dates*, as he would call them."

"I'm sure Zeke and my cousins have made this

abundantly clear, but it's worth repeating. You were held captive. While you knew what was going on, he made sure you had no power. It was an abusive situation. You have to stop looking at this as if you could have done anything to prevent it."

"Deep down I know he would have done the same thing to me that he did to Kate, but it doesn't change the fact that I feel like I should have known."

"I get that," Weston said. "I have to ask. Who's Kate?"

"A friend of mine who ended up dead in a hotel. Cause of death was ruled an overdose, but I know Bradly had her killed."

"How?"

"He all but told me." Haven held up her hand. "I can't prove it, but he made it crystal clear that would be my fate if I didn't do what I was told."

"I want to ask you one more question, and then we'll leave it alone for tonight."

"Okay."

"Did you ever meet Phil Wicker?"

Haven's eyes went wide. "Yes. Why?"

"He's the reason I was booted from the Army. But I can't prove it. Not yet anyway." Weston took the book and set it aside. "He's also had run-ins with my cousins, Brayden, and Zeke. The fact that his name is in that book makes me wonder if this thing just got a whole lot bigger than Bradly wanting to get back at you."

"Oh my God." She stared at him with fear etched in her eyes. "You haven't said anything to them about that book, have you?"

"Not yet. However, we need to first thing in the morning. Wicker's a CIA agent who has a lot of power. He fucked me over and thanks to him, my best friend is dead. My career and good name are trash. Wicker doesn't like my cousins. He likes me even less. If he knows his name is in that book and that the three of us are here… well, that spells trouble with a capital T."

"How would he know you're here?"

"It wouldn't take much to figure out where I might land. Bradly already knows who's protecting you. He's seen my face." Weston leaned over and tapped his finger on the book. "I'm sure Wicker isn't the only one in that book who's nervous, but he's the only one who has a connection to me, Ethan, and Rocky. And to you." Weston squeezed her leg. "I'll call Zeke in the morning. We can talk about it then." He took her by the hands and helped her off the sofa. "For now, try to get some sleep."

"I think that's going to be impossible." She

glanced over her shoulder. "Would you mind staying with me for a little while?"

"You mean like in your bed?"

"Maybe I can doze off with you there."

"If you think it will help."

Thankfully, Gunner followed them into the bedroom. Even better when he jumped up on the mattress.

Weston climbed in on the right side, tucking his feet up under Gunner's chin.

Haven snuggled in next to him, resting her head on his shoulder. "Thank you."

"Not a problem."

"I know it's silly. I mean, you were right in the other room, but I feel safer with you here."

"I'm not going to let anything happen to you."

"I'm sorry Wicker ruined your life," Haven said. "I've met him a few times and I don't like him. He's never treated the girls well. Bradly had promised me that he wouldn't tolerate clients who were pricks, but he never kept his word. Wicker put one of my friends in the hospital."

"Did she report it?"

"No." Haven sniffled. "Bradly wouldn't pay for her bills if she had. He threatened her before the doctor had even had the chance to examine her. A few weeks later I was able to help her leave, but I paid the price for that one."

Weston took her chin with his thumb and fore-finger. "I'm glad you were able to get her out, but I'm sorry he hurt you."

"I wanted to help more of the girls. I still do. I just don't know how. I've tried figuring out what his entries in that book mean, but I can't."

"We will." He pressed his lips against hers. He knew he shouldn't kiss her especially while tangled up under her sheets. The attraction to her was more than physical. She touched a part of his soul he thought had died years ago. He'd come to Fallport to mend fences and have an existence.

Now he wanted more. His heart demanded a life. A reason to do more than beat the blood through his body. It wanted to be whole again. To love.

A concept he hadn't thought about in years.

"I keep doing that," he whispered. "And I shouldn't."

"But it's nice."

"I won't disagree."

She wrapped her arms and legs around his body, resting her head on his chest.

It had been a long time since he held a woman in his arms for no other reason than to simply be close.

He struggled with human connection. The ability to be emotionally intimate had become impossible. Even after he'd chosen to change his ways with women, he still couldn't bring himself to get close to anyone. But with Haven, all his fears and insecurities melted away.

He couldn't pinpoint any one thing about her that drew him in. It certainly wasn't the drama. He normally avoided anyone with baggage. He had enough of that on his own and didn't need to date anyone with a set of problems like Haven.

However, he found himself wanting to not only protect her, but understand and care for her in ways only a loving partner could. It didn't make sense. This hadn't been part of his plan. As a matter of fact, it could screw with his future when it came to his family. Something he needed to consider.

He closed his eyes and did his best to ignore his personal desires. A lot had happened in a short period of time. He'd managed to restore some trust with Ethan and Rocky. That had been nothing short of a miracle. He didn't want to destroy that. But the more he thought about it, the more it angered him that they believed they had a right to dictate his love life. He could understand they were trying to protect Haven. But now that they had all the facts, they should know that he would never hurt her intentionally. He wasn't that man anymore.

"Weston?"

"Yes?" He pressed his lips to her temple.

"Your entire body just tensed. Why?"

He could lie, but that didn't seem right. Not if he wanted to truly turn over a new leaf. "I was just thinking about the situation we're in and how you were warned to stay away from me because of my past."

"I don't think it's only because of your reputation with women." She raised her head, pressing her chin to his shoulder.

"It has everything to do with what my cousins believed to be true about me and it's all based on half-truths." He brushed her hair from her face. "I'll admit I've behaved badly in many instances. But they misjudged me."

"They were just trying to protect me and given my past, you can't blame them." She covered his mouth. "There have been a lot of upstanding men in this community who have made assumptions about me because of the escort agency and because of what happened with Bradly. I've been propositioned and I've had assholes hit on me, expecting I would be an easy one-night stand."

"It's pretty unfair of them to believe I'd be like those men."

"Don't get mad, but if they believed you spent fourteen years not seeing your own kid, they would believe anything, and from what I heard during that conversation, you didn't try very hard to correct them. You played the black sheep like it was your duty."

He laughed. "To a certain extent, you're right. I did. But my family has always been all about action, not words. I tried to show them the kind of man I was becoming through my career. It fell on deaf ears."

"Sometimes you have to do both." She kissed his chest. "I'm still hoping my parents will see me, and then maybe they will talk to me. I keep writing them letters, hoping they will read them, but so far, they have not responded."

"I'm so sorry, babe. That's horrible."

"I hurt them and they're embarrassed by my actions. I get that. Hell, I'm mortified by what I did. Zeke keeps reminding me that it will take time for them to forgive me and themselves. But I don't think any of that can happen until Bradly is gone." She snuggled in closer, if that was possible. "You already have the past in your rearview. You have time and space on your side. Ethan and Rocky have shown you that they care and want a relationship. They wouldn't have trusted you with helping me or continued to let you stay here if that wasn't the case."

He had to admit she had a valid point. Things with his cousins had gone better than he expected. Everything was out in the open. However, he didn't want to do anything that would jeopardize those relationships. Haven was an unexpected complication that he wasn't sure how to handle. From the moment he laid eyes on her, he knew she was special. The more he spent time with her, the more he longed to have permanence in his life. His cousins didn't have the right to dictate who he dated. That wasn't fair. But he would respect their feelings for Haven and have a conversation with them before he let things with Haven go too far.

"How do you feel about going on a proper date with me?"

She popped her head up. In the moonlight shining through the window, he could see her blinking frantically. "Excuse me?"

"We're not working every night this week and I thought maybe I could take you out to dinner."

"In the middle of all this chaos, you want to date me?"

He laughed. "I like you."

"My past doesn't bother you?"

"No. It doesn't." He palmed her cheek and brushed his lips over her mouth. "Are you concerned about mine?"

"Do I know everything?"

"Of course not, but you know the things that should make you wonder if you're making a bad choice or not."

"When people in this town see us out together, they will gossip. And then they will pull you aside and warn you about me."

"I make my own judgments about people, and I certainly don't listen to bullshit gossip." He arched a brow.

"But some of it's true."

"I wish you would stop worrying about what everyone thinks."

"You know better than anyone that's no easy task. Have you been able to do that when it comes to your past? And be honest," she said.

"The only people I worry about are my family and those I want in my life. The people I value and respect. That's a small circle. Everyone else can go fuck themselves."

"Try that philosophy in your hometown." She

dropped her head to his chest and sighed. "I suspect they all still believe you're a deadbeat dad and would have something to say about that."

"And I don't give a shit. If they want to believe that about me, then they don't know me and I don't want them in my life. I know the truth and now my cousins do too. My parents will hear the truth soon enough. They matter to me and I want to mend fences with them as well. Outside of that, I only care about what you think and those I work with."

"My situation is different because there is truth to the rumors. You didn't do anything wrong. I did."

He understood why she felt the way she did. He supposed if he were in her shoes, he might have the exact same reaction. What he couldn't fathom was the poor treatment by everyone in this town. If they knew about the abuse, they should at least be able to empathize with how she ended up in the situation.

"The only mistake you made was to trust the wrong man," Weston said. "You're not the only woman to have made an error in judgment in that department." He kissed her forehead. "Get some sleep. I want to get up early and meet with my cousins and Zeke first thing."

She pulled the covers to her chin. "I've been avoiding giving them that book. They are going to want to share with Lewis and I don't want the cops involved."

"Lewis is on our side. We can trust him."

"You don't even know him."

"Is there something about him you think we should know?"

"No. He's a good man," she said. "I honestly believed that if I held on to the book, telling no one, Bradly would simply leave me alone. That he would realize I wasn't going to do anything with it."

"You know he's never going to let you go whether you give that book back or not."

"I know." She rolled to her side, tucking her ass against his hip, hugging his arm. "I've accepted that now. I'm just scared. I may be surrounded by very capable ex-military men, but Bradly is ruthless with no moral compass. He doesn't care who he hurts or what he has to do in order to get what he wants."

He wrapped his arms around her and kissed her neck. "We're not going to let him hurt you anymore."

"It might not be me he comes after."

Weston had considered that already. The best way to put the pressure on someone was to go after the people they loved the most. In this case, it would be her parents or possibly his cousins and Zeke.

Or worse, their families.

CHAPTER EIGHT

Haven avoided going anywhere in town. It was bad enough she had to deal with the stares and whispers at On the Rocks while she was working, but it was worse when she went anywhere else. At least at the bar, she had the camaraderie of Zeke and those she worked with who didn't judge her or if they did, they kept their thoughts to themselves.

She fiddled with a cup of coffee and did her best to enjoy the sunshine as the warmth hit her face, grateful the park wasn't filled with too many people. It could have been worse. Zeke could have suggested they meet at the diner or some other indoor place where it was more likely she could run into her parents or others who would glare at her as if she were some leper. Those who cared about her constantly told her that the people of Fallport would forget all about her sordid past, but she struggled to believe that concept.

Weston took her hand and squeezed it. "You look as though someone kicked your dog."

"I wish we had brought Gunner. Walking him is the only time I come out in public."

"After the altercation with Ted and people still believed I was Alexandra's father, I couldn't go anywhere without people commenting on my behavior. Or what they thought I should be doing. It didn't matter if I corrected them because they believed what they wanted, so I stopped trying."

"But you moved away."

"It took a couple of months before my transfer went through and the judge wanted to make sure I was serious about following through on the conditions he set forth. He took a really big risk with what he did. I struggled for the first few months. I lost friendships because of what I did, and because Darlene didn't want people to know she had an affair and that Alexandra was Ted's, she continued to let everyone believe she was mine. I understand what you're going through, and yes, I got to leave and start over somewhere else, but there has always been an emptiness in me regarding my family and close friends. I hate that some still think I'm a shitty person who would walk away from my child."

"Again, different because it's not true."

He pushed her sunglasses to the top of her head. "What is true is that I put a man in the hospital. I'm ashamed of that and always will be. I have to live with my actions. I was also dishonorably discharged from the military. While I know in my heart what I did on that mission didn't deserve that harsh punishment, it has brought shame to my family and to me. My best friend died in my arms. I can't get that image out of my head. I replay it constantly. I keep thinking about what I could have done differently to save him." He held her chin with his thumb and forefinger. "We all have a cross to bear. We all have something in our past that sits in our soul. But we don't have to let it taint our hearts. I'm choosing to end the madness that has shaped my adult life. You're so young and have so much to look forward to. Don't live the next ten years like I have." He wiped away a tear that dribbled down her cheek.

"I wish I knew how."

"You do it by living," he said. "You want to be an FBI agent or go into law enforcement, then do it. Don't let anyone or anything stand in your way. Change your mindset. You have the tools and the support." His soft, tender lips brushed over her mouth. He kissed her like she was the only person who mattered. It was filled with compassion and the kind of desire a man was supposed to have for a woman. It was sweet and made her want to experience all the things she thought she'd never have in her life.

Weston wasn't like anyone she'd ever met before. He was a contradiction at every turn. He was kind, sweet, and sensitive on one hand. On the other, he was fiercely protective and all man.

He deepened the kiss, wrapping his tongue around hers in an intoxicating dance.

Her head spun.

"Haven? What are you doing?" a familiar deep voice asked.

She jerked, dropping her coffee in her lap. "Shit." She glanced up, staring at her father.

Her mother gripped her dad's arm. She stared at her with wide eyes and shock oozing from her glare. It was the same look her mom used to give her when she'd done something wrong as a kid, only worse. This had all the judgment of a mother who had given up on her child.

"This isn't the place to being doing something like this," her father said.

"What exactly are you implying?" She swallowed hard. As a child, she would never dare to speak back to her father. Her parents were strict but loving. It was difficult for her growing up because they demanded she be something that she wasn't. They wanted an obedient daughter who believed in the same ideology that they did, but she wanted more from her life. It wasn't that she didn't want a family because she did. But she wanted a career, and she wanted it on her terms, not theirs.

Her father raised his palms. "I'm just saying you're in a public place and being with a man—"

"You don't know what you're talking about." She gritted her teeth.

"I know what I saw with my own two eyes." Her dad glared. "It's not appropriate and people will talk. Your actions have consequences. You need to think about what you're doing and how it will be perceived by everyone in this town."

"I have no idea who you are, but you have no right to speak to her that way." Weston stood, puffing out his chest.

Her dad laughed. "I can speak to my daughter any way I want to, young man. This doesn't concern you."

"Weston." She curled her fingers around his biceps but kept her ass on the park bench. "Let it be."

"Absolutely not," Weston said. "I don't care who he is, I'm not going to stand here and let anyone chastise you."

"That's not what I'm doing," her father said with a sarcastic tone. "I don't know if you have any idea about her past, but I'm honestly trying to look out for my child. People here have a long memory and will gossip."

Weston growled. It was a menacing noise, much like her dog made when a stranger came knocking on the door. "That's bullshit. If you took the time to read Haven's letters or have a goddamned conversation with her to hear the truth about what happened, you'd know that."

"This is none of your business," her mother said. "Haven, we'd like to talk with you, in private, please."

"Excuse me?" Haven blinked. "Why now? For two months you've ignored me."

"We have our reasons," her father said. "Haven, please. We need to chat."

"You don't know the half of what she's been through. Shame on you for not hearing her or seeing her for who she really is. I feel sorry for you. You're missing out on knowing a kind, loving, wonderful human."

Her father looked Weston up and down. "You have a real chip on your shoulder, young man."

"Not the first time I've heard that. I think you need to leave," Weston said.

Her father took her mother by the arm. "Haven, it's important that we talk, but this obviously isn't the right time. We'll be in touch." Her parents strolled off toward the entrance of the park.

Weston shook out his hands. "I'm sorry. I probably shouldn't have spoken to your parents like that."

She jumped to her feet and wrapped her arms around his strong shoulders. "Thank you. No one has ever stood up for me like that before." She kissed him, hard and with intent.

He cupped her face, prying her lips from his long before she wanted it to end. "I'm sure my cousins and Zeke have defended you," he whispered.

"They've never had to with my parents. They don't come into the bar and to my knowledge, when their paths have crossed, no words have been exchanged, at least not bad ones." Tears burned her eyes.

"Hey. I'm sorry. I didn't mean to make you cry."

"I don't understand why you're pushing me

away." Of all the people in her life, Weston had shown her hope that she could have a normal life, something she wasn't sure could ever be possible.

He pulled her tight to his chest. "Trust me, that's the last thing I want to do. I just know I'm not the only one standing in your corner." He smiled before kissing her softly.

She melted into his arms, caving to his tender touch. He made her feel cared for and safe. As if there was truly a light at the end of the tunnel that had been so dark for so long. Before Weston had strolled into town, she honestly thought she'd have to sneak out in the middle of the night. That disappearing would be the only answer. But running would mean she'd forever be looking over her shoulder, waiting for Bradly to find her, and that would only mean one thing.

Her death.

"Excuse us," Ethan said with a dark tone.

Weston jumped, stuffing his hands into his pockets. "Oh. Hey. I didn't see you there."

Zeke chuckled.

"I suspect you didn't," Rocky said with a grim expression. He held up a bag. "We brought doughnuts."

"Wonderful, because I'm starving." Haven

snagged the bag. "We ran into my parents and it was weird, to say the least." She swiped at her cheeks.

"Her folks want to have a chat with her and it freaked her out. I was just comforting Haven," Weston said.

"It looked like something else from our vantage point." Ethan pointed to a picnic table. "Why don't you and Zeke take these over there. I want to have a word with my cousin."

Haven glared.

Zeke wrapped his arm around her shoulders. "Come on. Let's give them a little space."

"I don't think so." She dug her heels into the ground. "Not if they're going to give him a lecture when one isn't deserving."

"It's fine." Weston nodded. "We'll be over in a second."

Begrudgingly, Haven let Zeke guide her across the grass. "What is their problem with Weston? I thought they moved past their issues."

"For the most part I believe they have, but we're all worried about you and we all asked him to keep his distance. He obviously hasn't done that."

She tilted her head. "It's not any of your business whom I hang out with."

Zeke arched a brow. "He's supposed to be protecting you, not playing house."

"That's not what we're doing." She plopped herself down at the table and opened the bag, pulling out a chocolate treat. "I like him. He's kind and he doesn't judge me like everyone else in this godforsaken town."

"I'm glad about that, but are you sure you want a romantic entanglement right about now?" Zeke straddled the bench across from her and gave her that damn big brother look that made her want to crawl right out of her skin. She knew he meant well, but that still didn't make her feel any better about the situation.

"I don't know, but it's for me and Weston to decide. Not you three goons."

"Fair enough. However, you need to let the three of them work out their family shit on their own. They're big boys and at the end of the day, Ethan and Rocky are only trying to look out for you—and Weston." Zeke reached across the table and took her hand. "For the record, I like Weston. I see how he looks at you and vice versa. I have no doubt his intentions are good, but the timing sucks."

"I won't disagree with that statement." She

glanced toward the sun, lowering her sunglasses back over her eyes.

"So, your parents blew through, huh? That couldn't have been fun."

"It wasn't the worst, but they gave me mixed messages, which I don't understand." She nibbled on the pastry. "But Weston, he stood right up to my dad. Only, at one point, I was afraid he might toss a punch."

"That's one thing that Rocky and Ethan are always afraid of when it comes to Weston. As a teenager, he was a bit of a hothead. Always getting in fights at school and over dumb shit too."

"Well, Weston held himself together."

"I'm glad to hear it and I'm sorry your folks weren't kind."

"But they weren't necessarily mean." She glanced over her shoulder. "I hope Rocky and Ethan aren't too hard on Weston. I don't want him backing off because his cousins have their heads up their collective asses."

"If they are, I promise to have a chat with them."

"Thank you." She finished her treat, grateful for the sugar rush. "If we can get rid of Bradly, I'd like to see where this might take me. Outside of you and them, Weston is the only normal thing in my life."

* * *

Weston braced himself for the tongue-lashing. He leaned against a tree and tried to keep his frustration in check. This wasn't the place for the past to rear its ugly head. But he wasn't a child anymore. This couldn't be compared to when he got caught with Riley Simpson behind the shed when she'd been dating someone else in the family. Boy, that hadn't gone over well. The worst part had been she'd told everyone that Weston had kissed her without her permission, which wasn't true. Riley had initiated contact. That incident had been the beginning of his family believing he was a womanizing prick and he'd only been seventeen.

His father had been furious and he'd successfully made his mother cry.

Rocky and Ethan had been visiting that weekend, and they tore into him like a raging wildfire. It did matter what Weston said about the incident. Everyone believed Riley's version.

Story of Weston's life.

"What the hell are you doing?" Rocky asked. "We told you she was off-limits and we come to the park and find you in a lip-lock."

"Nothing has happened," Weston said. "Other

than a couple of kisses." Jesus, he felt like a twelve-year-old, which just pissed him off. Outside of work and this particular protection detail, he didn't answer to his cousins. His personal life was none of their fucking business. However, he did respect Rocky and Ethan and he wanted to talk to them about his feelings. But not like this.

"Are you joking? That's not nothing." Ethan bent over and picked up a stick, tossing it across the park. "We thought you changed."

"I have and I resent you coming in this hot without listening to what I have to say. Not to mention having any consideration for Haven or her feelings." Weston held up his hand. "I care about her and I had every intention of having a conversation with the two of you about exactly this before I took her out on a date."

"Getting involved with anyone is the last thing she needs." Rocky shook his head.

"It's not your decision to make. It's hers. And mine. I hear you and I understand your concerns," Weston said.

Ethan arched a brow. "We trusted you and now—"

"You can still trust me.' Weston couldn't believe he was still having this kind of conversation with his cousins. It seemed ridiculous, even under the circumstances surrounding Haven. "It's not like I wanted to have real feelings for her, but I can't turn them off. I've tried ignoring them." Weston squared his shoulders.

"Well, try harder," Ethan said.

"It's not that easy when she throws herself in my arms and plants one on my lips."

Rocky chuckled. "Yeah. We saw that."

Weston blinked. "What?"

"We were on the far side of the park when her parents walked away," Ethan said. "We watched the whole encounter."

"Then why the hell are you berating me if you knew I wasn't the one who instigated that kiss?" Weston wiggled his fingers.

"Two reasons." Rocky held up his two fingers. "Because you didn't stop her and because it's fun," Rocky said. "But we're still a little pissed. She doesn't need this in her life right now, and frankly, neither do you. She needs to get Bradly out of her life, get herself back in school, and mend relationships. You have your own set of issues to deal with."

"The fate of my future is in the hands of Fenmore and a new review board. The rest is up to my parents and the rest of our family."

"Have you spoken to anyone?" Ethan asked.

"I sent my folks a copy of the birth certificate. My dad called me this morning." Weston dropped his head back to the tree and glanced to the sky.

"How'd that go?" Rocky asked.

"Well enough." Weston lowered his chin, glancing between his cousins. "They want to come out for a visit."

"That's good," Ethan said. "I'm glad that fences are being mended. But that doesn't change the fact that we don't believe getting involved in a romantic situation with Haven is a good idea for either one of you."

"That's not for you to decide." Weston pushed from the tree. "I like her."

"We noticed," Rocky said. "But we need you focused, especially now that you've seen the book, which is the real reason we wanted to talk with you."

"Why didn't you just say that?" Weston asked. Sometimes his cousins could be royal pains in the ass.

"You mentioned in the text we should speak privately before we all met, but that didn't happen. So let's do it now," Ethan said. "Bradly's touring that office building as we speak. I don't know if it's smoke and mirrors, or if he's serious about bringing a business here. Either way, we have to stop him. Haven needs peace in her life so she can have a chance in this town."

"I couldn't tell if her parents were coming around or wanted to give her hell." Weston knew a little about that. His mom and dad judged him harshly on every front as a kid, but they loved him dearly. Sometimes it was justified, other times not so much. They might have been disappointed in the way his life had turned out, but they never cut off communication completely. He'd been the one—out of shame—who'd stopped coming around.

"We don't know them well, but what we do know is they are incredibly traditional, old-fashioned, and religious," Rocky said. "Time and her showing them she's still their daughter are the only things that are going to help that relationship."

"And maybe if everyone else in this town gets behind her," Weston mumbled. "There is way too much victim shaming and even she won't admit she was a victim."

"Tell us something we don't know." Rocky threaded his fingers through his beard. "You've seen the book, right? What can you tell us?"

"There are a few names in it that I recognize, or have come across in my career, but the one that stands out is Wicker and he's mentioned more than once." Weston figured it was best to cut to the chase.

"You've got to be fucking kidding me." Rocky's face hardened. "That man's like a bad rash."

"He ruined my career," Weston said.

"Did you ask Haven about Wicker?"

"She knows he's the reason I got booted from the Army and does know who he is. But outside of that, I didn't get into details. I wanted you to see the book before we pressed her too hard."

"Maybe you dating Haven isn't such a bad idea after all," Rocky said.

"Nope. No way. I'm not playing double agent." Weston shook his head. "I care about her too much to lie to her about anything. But I won't lie to the two of you either. Having you back in my life in a positive way means too much."

"Who are you and what have you done with our pansy-ass little cousin?" Ethan laughed. "All right. I want to make a copy of the book and then put the original in a safe."

"That makes the most sense." Weston nodded.

"Anything else we should know about it?" Rocky asked.

"She created the book, but Bradly made entries that don't make sense to her. I think it's a code, but I haven't been able to crack it. However, the biggest concern we have is the powerhouse of people that are in it. I know from Haven most are clients. But some of the girls are women who worked for Bradly and they are the daughters of some very powerful men and women in Washington. I do believe this book is just one way Bradly extorts those who have used his services. He could destroy some pretty influential people in the FBI, the CIA, in Washington, and even in the military."

"This is a clusterfuck," Ethan mumbled. "And above our pay grade."

"What about the agent helping with my case?" Weston asked. "I bet she could be helpful, especially since she wants to nail Wicker and whoever is above him. I think it's personal for her, but I don't know that for a fact."

"Brayden really liked her. He had nothing but good things to say. After we go through it with Haven, let's give her a call," Ethan said. "I'd like to hear her point of view."

"Sounds like a plan." Weston stole a glance at Haven and smiled. "Now, about this dating thing. I do want your blessing. It means something to me."

"Hurt her, and we'll break your legs." Rocky slapped his back.

"What if she hurts me?" It had been a long time since Weston had let his guard down with a woman and in less than a week, he'd done just that with Haven.

"We're not concerned with that." Ethan laughed. "Just kidding. We'll give her a stern talking to and then find her someone better."

"You two are unbelievable." Weston chuckled. Never in a million years did he think he'd be joking like this with his cousins, but it felt like home.

CHAPTER NINE

Haven rubbed her eyes. The last two hours had been not only emotionally grueling, but it made her bone-tired. Her muscles ached as if she'd run a marathon at full sprint.

Weston stood and scooted in on her side of the booth. He wrapped his arm around her shoulders. "You doing okay?"

"That was a lot," she admitted. "I know you and your cousins are looking out for me, trying to find a way to nail Bradly, but it felt a little like I was being interrogated."

"We just need to find a way to use that book against Bradly and not necessarily against everyone that's in it," Weston said. "Brayden believes—and I agree—the information in the back is either bribes, blackmail, or both, especially after some of what you told us."

"Bradly is the master of manipulation. He has an uncanny way of finding a person's weak spot and exploiting it. With me, he knew I needed money and to feel like I was a capable human since my parents constantly squashed my aspirations under the pretense of caring about me."

"Some of the men in that book aren't any different than Bradly. I know this from personal experience."

"Are you speaking about Wicker?"

"I know a couple of other people, but yeah. Mostly him."

"If Bradly makes the connection between you and Wicker, he'll use it to destroy you." She lowered her gaze. Looking back, she could see every stupid mistake she'd made. While she understood there came a point where she was no longer in control, there were other ways she could have survived college. She chose to take the quick, easy cash.

Dumb move.

Weston laughed. "There's nothing he can do to me that hasn't already been done." He lifted her chin. "Bradly has no power over me; if he thinks he does, he's making a grave mistake. I am a man with nothing to lose."

"That's not true and he'll find a way to exploit your past." She blinked out a tear. "He'll dig up everything."

"Every indiscretion in my life is out in the open. There are no ugly secrets left. There's only one way he can hurt me, and that's if he hurts you." He tenderly brushed his lips over her mouth. Every time Weston kissed her, she felt a little surge of confidence shoot through her veins. She wanted to hold on to that feeling. Bottle it and save it for when she was alone. She knew getting it from a man wasn't the way to become the woman she once was, or the woman she wanted to be.

But it helped.

"We're calling Fenmore this afternoon," he said. "We're hoping she'll have some insight."

"Do you really think bringing in the FBI is a good idea?"

"My cousins and Zeke have tried doing this with the local police and their connections," Weston said. "But we need help to end this. When I texted with Fenmore to set up the call, she told me there is a case file on Bradly. It's not her case because she works military review, but she knows the agent working on it. She is going to have a chat with him before we call. She's our best bet."

Haven's cell buzzed. She pulled it from her purse and gasped. "Oh my God."

"What's wrong?"

"It's my mom." Haven stared at the text, reading it three times. "My dad's in the hospital. He was hit by a car after shoving my mom out of the way. She wants me to come to the emergency room right away." She lifted her gaze. "She wants me to bring one of my friends."

Weston grabbed her hand, yanking her from the booth. "I'll drive."

"Why does she want me there? Or one of you guys?" Her body shook from the inside out. She stared into Weston's caring eyes. "They hate me and it's obvious what she thinks of you and the rest of the guys."

He cupped her face. "I don't believe for one second that they hate you. Like my parents, they aren't looking at the whole picture. They could even be angry at themselves. But we won't know what's going on until we get there."

"I'm scared, Weston," she said with a shaky voice. "They've been so cruel ever since I've returned—until today."

"Babe, I know you're hurting and worried about what you're walking into. But maybe this is the beginning of a fresh start."

"I've wanted their forgiveness, but I'm not sure I can give it to them. Today at the park confused me. I didn't know if my folks were being passive-aggressive, or if they really want to have an honest chat. I'm angry and I don't understand why. I should be concerned for my dad."

"Everything you're feeling is normal."

She let out a sarcastic laugh. "Nothing about this is conventional. There's a part of me that doesn't want to go, if only to teach them a lesson in what it's like to feel as though the people who are supposed to care about you the most, don't."

"I know that feeling, babe. I've tried punishing my family, but it doesn't work that way. Text your mom and tell her we're on our way. I'll let Zeke know what's going on. It will leave him shorthanded, but I'm sure he'll understand."

"Thanks." She nodded. "I don't know how I'd get through this without you."

"I know you'd be just fine if I wasn't in the picture. You're a strong, confident woman. It took a lot of courage to leave Bradly. Even more to stay gone. I'm just the lucky bastard who will hopefully get to steal a few more kisses along the way."

"That has to be the sappiest thing I've ever heard."

He chuckled. "Yeah, it was pretty corny, but I've never met anyone like you before and I find myself wanting something I thought I'd never want again."

She opened her mouth, but no words formed. Zeke told her that someday, when everything blew over, she'd be able to move forward. That she could be and have anything she wanted, including a partner. She didn't believe him, but staring into Weston's unwavering gaze, she wondered if she'd stumbled into the one person in the world who wouldn't hold her past hostage. "We barely know each other," she whispered.

"Are you saying you don't feel the same way?"

"No, but to be honest, I'm struggling to trust it's real."

He cupped the back of her neck, pressing his lips firmly against her mouth. His tongue found its way to hers, swirling tenderly.

The tension in her body slowly lifted from her muscles as she sank into his strong frame, his arms wrapping tightly around her shoulders.

"Is that real enough for you?"

"There's this tape I play in my head. It started

before I met you. I actually went out on a date once about a month ago. I thought it might bring normalcy to my life." She spoke so fast she could barely catch her breath. "It was this guy who used to work here and he was nice. At first, he acted like he didn't care about my past and I believed him, but the reality was he couldn't get past the whispers and glares he got from everyone in this town. It got so bad after one date, he quit and moved."

"That's on him, not you." Weston smiled. "I'm used to people giving me a sideways stare. I don't care what people think of me, except for those I care about. I'm not going anywhere, except the emergency room. I think we should get a move on."

She nodded. "I'll go get my backpack." She turned and headed for the back room with her heart in her throat. Zeke, Ethan, or Rocky would have been right by her side. Their friendship had made living in Fallport bearable. Their protection made her feel safe.

But Weston gave her something they couldn't. She'd allowed Bradly to take away everything that made her a woman. She'd been to four therapy sessions and her doctor had told her it would take time to regain her confidence as a sexual woman, but that it would happen. That there was no reason she couldn't have a healthy relationship. She had the tools. Her therapist told her all the same things that Weston had. That she'd been a victim. Accepting that would give her the power to be one no longer.

She finally understood that concept.

HAVEN PAUSED at the curtain separating her from her parents. Nurses and doctors shuffled past. The smell of antiseptic filled her nostrils. The last time Haven had been in the hospital had been when Bradly beat her so badly he'd broken two ribs along with her arm, but managed to leave her face intact.

Asshole.

She squared her shoulders and sucked in a deep breath. No matter what had transpired between her and her parents, she certainly didn't wish for anything bad to happen.

"Do you want me to wait out here for a moment?" Weston asked.

"No." She wasn't ready to see them alone. "My mom specifically asked me to bring one of my friends. I don't know if that's because they don't want to be around me or because they need help due to what happened. Either way, I'd really like it if you didn't leave my side, even if they ask you to."

"Whatever you need. I'm here for you." He kissed her cheek. He was like a sweet angel sent from heaven—if she believed in that, which she didn't.

For most of her life, her philosophy was built around karma. What you put out in the world came back. That's why she was so hard on herself about her life choices.

It was time to stop stewing in the bad ones.

"Mom?" Haven pulled back the curtain. Tears burned her eyes like glue stuck in her sockets. Her father was hooked up to machines that beeped. An oxygen mask covered his mouth. An IV bag dripped drugs and fluids into his system. He had a cast on his right leg and left arm. His face was bruised and scraped and his eyes were swollen shut.

Her mom rested her head on the bed, holding her dad's hand. She lifted her gaze. "Oh, Haven." She rose slowly. Her eyes were bloodshot, and she had scratches and bruises on her face and arms. "Thank you for coming." Her mother reached out and squeezed her arm. It was a gentle, almost loving touch.

Haven swallowed a guttural sob. "I stopped at the nurses' station, and they told me Dad was stable, but he had a collapsed lung and a few broken bones."

"He's going to be okay, thank God. I gave the

police all the information I could, but it wasn't much." Her mom wiped her eyes. "I didn't see or hear the car coming. By the time I lifted my head from the pavement, the vehicle had already turned the corner."

"Were there any other witnesses?" Weston asked.

Her mom sighed. "Unfortunately, not that I'm aware of. I called 9-1-1 and kept my focus on Lee once I noticed no one was around."

"The police will comb the area, asking if anyone saw what happened," Weston said.

"You're the young man we saw this morning." Her mom took her father's hand and leaned against the gurney. "Weston, was it?"

"Yes, Mom. He's Rocky and Ethan's cousin. He works for the search and rescue team as well as helping Zeke out at the bar." Haven wanted to add that he was there to help her get rid of the man who had ruined her life, but she thought better of bringing that up.

"Pamela mentioned you." Her mom held Weston's gaze. "I'm Amanda, Haven's mom."

"I'm sorry about what happened," Weston said.

"I wouldn't believe anything Pamela has to say about any topic," Haven mumbled.

"She is a piece of work." Her mother laughed.

"She and her mother have been getting under my skin lately."

Haven grabbed Weston's forearm. All the air in her lungs escaped like a flock of birds. Elizabeth, Pamela's mother, has always considered herself one of Fallport's best citizens. She volunteered on numerous committees with Haven's mother and always had to be the one in charge. Elizabeth believed she was the best one to run anything because her family had been in Fallport forever. She did her best to rewrite her ancestry, making their history seem as though they'd never done a shitty thing, ever.

And then there was the church Haven's family attended. Elizabeth was the high-and-mighty type. She demanded her children not only be the best in anything they did, but they could also do no wrong, even when they did.

"Why, what has she been doing?" Haven asked, although she wasn't sure why, with the exception she knew her mother cared what people thought about her and her family.

Her mom fell back into the chair. Tears poured out her eyes like a raging river. "This has been so hard on your father and me. I can't imagine what it's been like for you."

Haven stole a glance at Weston. This was not the mother who had berated her when she'd first returned to Fallport. It gave Haven whiplash. "It totally sucks, Mom. But I honestly don't want to talk about that. I want to know what happened to Dad."

"Can you get my phone?" Her mom pointed to the portable tray on the other side of the bed. "I need to show your friend a few things. I haven't let Lewis see it yet."

"Why not?" Weston asked.

"I have no idea if it's related to what happened. We wanted to show it to you and Haven first. We've received threats about exposing Haven's past before. We ignored them in part because we won't be bullied, and also, it's not like everyone in this town hasn't made up their mind over what they think about it."

"You included," Haven said with more venom laced to her words than intended. "I'm sorry, Mom. But you and Dad have been ruthless ever since I took the job at the escort agency."

"I'm not disagreeing with you." Her mom lowered her head. "I don't know what I'm more ashamed of. Not being there for you when you needed us most or judging you for something we chose not to understand."

Haven gasped. This was the last thing she expected to hear from her parents. "Why have you not responded to my letters?"

"At first we were angry," her mother said between sobs. "Ashamed. Our daughter left college to work at an escort agency. We thought we raised you better than that. And then we learned…" Her mother covered her face. "We thought the worst of you without hearing your side of things. It wasn't until Elizabeth and Pamela started spreading horrible stories about you that we knew weren't true."

"I know this isn't my place." Weston leaned against the windowsill. "But considering how you believed the worst in the past, why was what they said different?"

"I'm so disgusted with myself for not understanding how this Bradly man abused my child." Her mother shook her head wildly. "But Pamela and her mother went on about how they knew of men in this town taking money for… for… I can't even say it and I know it's not true." She shifted, catching Haven's gaze, tears streaming down her cheeks. "I should have known that you would never willingly do what that man is trying to say you did." She raised her phone. "He's been sending us messages for weeks now. Telling us things about you. Horrible things. With pictures to go with it."

Haven took her mother's cell in her shaky hand. Her heart dropped to the pit of her stomach as she scrolled through the endless images and emails. If she'd seen them, in the context in which they were written, she'd believe Bradly too.

"Weston, take a look," Haven said.

"We don't understand what he wants, other than sending these horrible images out in the world. At first, we figured either the images were already circulating somewhere—"

"No offense, but that's not fair." Weston pushed from the window and took the cell. He stood at the end of the bed, scrolling through all the embarrassing images that documented Haven's devastating past.

Her in the arms of men. Taking money. Entering hotels. It didn't matter that they were classy establishments; she was there to perform sexual acts for money. There were even naked pictures of her with men, doing unspeakable things. All the proof her parents needed to know that the rumors were fact.

"And a little cowardice," Weston added.

"Maybe so." Her mom narrowed her eyes. "Do you have children?"

"No, ma'am, I don't. And I mean no disrespect by this, but I have parents who misjudged me and my actions. It's been a constant struggle to maintain a relationship, something that I want." Weston squeezed Haven's hand. "I'm speaking out of turn, but I know that's what Haven wants with you."

Her mother ran her hand up and down her father's arm, glancing between him and Haven. "Being a parent isn't easy. Kids don't come with instructions. We only wanted what we thought was best for you. We thought a little tough love when you started working at that agency might help you realize it was a mistake."

"We need to go back to what happened before that, Mom." Haven pulled the other chair closer. Her belly filled with the same heavy bricks that normally made it impossible for her to have an adult conversation with her mother. Being around her folks, she tended to revert back to her rebellious sixteen-year-old self who wanted to be anything other than the perfect little girl her parents had envisioned. "You wanted me to change my major. You demanded it. You refused to help me at all unless I did."

"Are you trying to say what happened is our fault, because we—"

"No, Mom." Tentatively, Haven rested her hand

over her mother's. "I don't blame you for anything that happened. I know my decision to take that job was a bad one. I didn't know that at the time, nor did I have any idea when I first met Bradly that he'd turn out to be a monster. However, I had to work to pay for school and the jobs I had weren't enough. Once you and Dad decided to take away what little help you could afford to give me, I had to make other choices because at first, I didn't want to leave school. Being in law enforcement was all I ever wanted."

"It's so dangerous. We didn't want that for our baby," her mother whispered, holding up her hand. "Your father and I have been talking a lot about this and we're seeing that maybe we made a mistake in pushing our wants and dreams on you, instead of listening to what you really wanted."

"Wow. I can't believe you're saying all this." Haven leaned back. "Why were you so mean in the park this morning?"

"We were surprised to see you in the embrace of a man, considering whoever has been sending us those things, demanding we tell you to give back whatever it is you took, or those things go public."

"Why didn't you come to Haven sooner?" Weston asked. "Or my cousins. Or Zeke?"

"I could come up with a million reasons, but

none of them make sense anymore." Her mom leaned over and pressed the back of her hand to her father's cheek. "Do you think this could be connected?"

"Bradly is a dangerous man," Weston said. "He'll stop at nothing to get what he wants, including hurting the people whom Haven cares about most. So yes, it's the only thing that makes sense." He waved the phone. "Do you mind if I forward all these to myself?"

Her mom shook her head. "I need to know how you got to a place in your life where you felt you need to sell…" She covered her face.

Haven closed her eyes and counted to ten before blinking them open. She wasn't sure if this was the right place or not to have this conversation, but her mom had gone from not wanting to have anything to do with her, to asking the hard questions, with real caring emotion.

"I'll give you ladies some space." Weston squeezed her shoulder. "I need to make a few phone calls anyway." He bent over and kissed her temple. "Call me if you need me."

"Thanks." She glanced over her shoulder and stared at the backside of Weston as he pulled back the curtain and strolled out into the corridor.

"He seems like a nice young man." Her mom let out a long breath. "How long have you been dating him?"

Oh boy. That was a strong word and Haven wasn't sure how to answer. "It's new."

"You're lucky to have a man like him."

"You don't even know him, Mom." Shit. There was no reason for her to be so combative. "But yeah, I am."

Her mom nodded. "I know this is all painful, but please make me understand what happened."

"I don't know if I can do that in a single conversation. It's complicated." Haven took her mother's hand. "But it's not your fault if that's what you're thinking."

"You were always such a stubborn, strong-willed child. I worried about you so much when you went off to college, but never in a million years did I think you'd get involved in something like that." Her mom sniffled. "Your father and I believed you'd always make the most out of a tough situation because of how smart and resourceful you are."

"I appreciate the props, Mom. I really do. The only way I know how to explain it is to say that I got greedy when it came to the money aspect when the escort agency was legit."

"Can those places really be that way?"

"They can and this one was aboveboard. But then this guy, Bradly—the one we believe is emailing you and Dad—took advantage of me." As the words fell off her tongue, she understood just how much of a victim she'd really been. She could see with such clarity how she'd fallen into the hands of a predator. She didn't stand a chance. "Before I knew what hit me, I was in an abusive relationship with an older man. I didn't see a way out."

"I'm so sorry we weren't there for you. Is there any chance you could see it in your heart to forgive us and start fresh?"

This was everything she wanted and yet, she had no idea how to respond. There was a part of her that didn't trust her mother's words. It wasn't just the last two months; it was years of struggles and pain.

"I've been seeing a therapist. Would you be willing to go with me?" Haven asked.

"We'd be open to that." Her mom smiled weakly.

"I do need to ask you something."

"What, dear?"

"You've always been so concerned about what people think and right now, this town has a pretty low opinion of me. How will that factor into us healing our relationship?"

Her mother laughed. It was sweet, genuine, and full of life. "That won't be a problem anymore, especially after I told Elizabeth to go fuck herself."

Haven covered her mouth. "Mother. You just dropped the F-bomb."

"I know. But if you think you're shocked, you should have seen Elizabeth. Talk about stunned. I've never seen that woman speechless before. It was utterly priceless." Her mom leaned forward, wrapping her arms around Haven. "I want my daughter back and I'm willing to do whatever it takes to make that happen."

CHAPTER TEN

Haven stepped from the bathroom. Every bone in her body ached. Her mind filtered through the past and present like a twister racing down the road, destroying everything in its path. The overwhelming sense of doom filled her soul. The weight of it all made it difficult to move forward. She inched closer to the kitchen.

Weston sat at the table. A massive amount of paperwork was sprawled across the top. He rubbed his temples before glancing over his shoulder. "Hey, babe, did you have a nice shower?"

"I wish I had a bathtub." She leaned over and kissed his cheek. "What's all this?" She pulled up a chair and tapped her fingers on a stack of papers.

"All the intel that Fenmore sent over. The pages

from your book. Stuff that Brayden and my cousins gave me. I'm trying to make sense of it all, but it's a tall order. I feel like I'm out of my lane. I'm used to sitting on a hill with a rifle, waiting patiently to fire. I'm the guy who follows orders. I don't plan missions or analyze data. My job has never been to solve the mystery, but to eliminate the threat."

"Maybe I can help."

"I'm not supposed to show you half of it." He leaned back and ran a hand across the top of his head.

"That just pisses me off."

"I didn't say you couldn't see it; I'm just repeating what I was told."

"Why doesn't anyone want me looking at it?" She pushed her chair back and went to the cupboard, pulling down two glasses. She snagged a bottle of wine and poured. She handed him one before leaning against the counter and taking a generous swig. "I'm not a child. This affects me more than it does anyone else."

"They want to protect you."

"That's lame if you ask me. What's on those pages can't hurt me. Only Bradly and his goons can."

"I couldn't agree more, so why don't you sit your adorable ass back down and help me with this shit, because I don't have a clue as to what I'm looking at."

"Well, when it you put it like that, how can I refuse?" She forced a smile, even though everything in her world felt as though it was about to get worse, not better.

He pushed a file across the table. "This is the active case against Wicker."

"What are they looking into him for?"

"A plethora of things, but the one they are building the strongest case against him for is similar to mine where it led to the deaths of five Navy SEALs that were working with a JSOC team, only the JSOC team made it out, untouched. As a matter of fact, their paths never crossed due to misinforma-tion on the ground. Or bad communication. The report is unclear."

She pushed her glass aside and flipped open the file. "What is his end game?"

"I have no idea outside of greed," Weston said.

"Do they believe he's a double agent?"

"That's just it. Fenmore doesn't think so. She has no evidence that he's been selling anything to our enemies. But that doesn't mean he's not taking money somewhere. In the case you're looking at, the SEALs were ambushed by a Columbian drug cartel.

Fenmore thinks he was helping them move product and that team was in his way. What they don't understand is why the JSOC team didn't move in. That's what doesn't make sense."

"But wouldn't selling or buying drugs from a cartel and moving it into our country by a CIA agent still be considered treason or something?"

Weston pursed his lips. "It's something all right. What we need to find is that connection to Bradly."

"Well, that's easy. Wicker's a client. A regular."

"Not enough." Weston lifted a piece of paper. "There are eight names on this list from the CIA. Three of which I know personally. I didn't see their names right away because they were in the middle of the book and I was so focused on Wicker. But just because they used the escort agency isn't enough of a connection. Of course, my gut feeling on this could be all wrong. Just because Wicker's name is listed in your book more than others and Bradly's contribution to the book has an asterisk by his name—and two others have it—doesn't tell us anything."

"Why do you believe Wicker's more involved in Bradly's business?"

"Because the agent working on the case uncovered that Wicker is listed as an investor in one of Bradly's shell companies. One that deals with foreign trade. It's a conflict of interest and was flagged two years ago. However, it's been a struggle to prove any wrongdoing."

Haven lifted her gaze. "I don't know anything about Bradly's other businesses except the money laundering. I know he has them along with investments in oil, IT, and other corporations, but he made me stay in my lane. My job was to match the client with the right girl."

"Who was Wicker matched with?"

"That's an interesting question."

Weston arched a brow as he rested his hands on the table. His unwavering stare rattled her nerves. He held her gaze. It wasn't judgmental, but it still sent a chill up her spine. She couldn't explain why. It wasn't as if he'd never given her this expression before. Perhaps she read too much into the situation. Her insecurities often got the better of her when it came to discussing anything having to do with the escort agency or her time with Bradly.

"More interesting than other clients? And why?"

"Because I never matched him."

"I'm sorry, but I don't understand how any of this works. Can you explain it to me?"

Haven rolled her neck. No one had ever asked her this before and she wasn't prepared to get into the nitty-gritty of it all. A brick dropped to the center of her gut. The thump, thump, thump of her heart filled her ears like the roar of the rain pelting against a window. "When the agency was still legit, customers would ask for certain attributes. Eye and hair color. Height. Age. Even intelligence in certain subjects. We would do our best to match them with the appropriate girl. When Bradly took over, it became more about what the client wanted in the bedroom. The hard part about that was many of the girls didn't really know what they were getting into." She turned her head, avoiding eye contact. The shame was heavier than an elephant sitting on her chest.

"Just like you." Weston squeezed her knee.

"Yes," she whispered. "Only, I knew what I was sending them into and I did very little to stop it."

"I want you to stop focusing on all the things that you believe you did wrong and remember how much Bradly controlled you through fear and violence. You did what you had to do in order to survive. Everyone else has their own story. There are some girls there by their own choice and others are like you. But you can't take responsibility for all of them. However, you can help put an end to it now."

Slowly, her narrative had shifted. At least when it

came to her own actions and how Bradly had her trapped inside an invisible prison. She might not have been able to see the bars, but she could feel them as if he'd tied a noose around her neck. However, the guilt over how she treated those who worked at the agency tightened the noose, suffocating her, killing her spirit. "It's not easy to do that sometimes." She squared her shoulders, sucking in a deep breath. Weston was right. She had to look at what she could do, not what she hadn't done.

"If you didn't set up Wicker with a girl, who did?" Weston asked.

"No one, that's the problem. All dates were paired by me. Sometimes Bradly would make adjustments."

"But Wicker is in the book and you mentioned you knew he was a client. That makes no sense."

"There are three clients that I called Ghost Clients. Wicker was one. George Thompson and James Gorgen are the other two. Those asterisks that you noted. I took their initial information. Put them into the system. Wrote their names in the book. But I never set them up with a girl. Bradly would call me at the office, tell me to add a girl's name to each of the men in our system. As if the date happened. I was then told to pay the girls. I got curious and asked one of them and they told me they got a call from Bradly directly to go to a location for a VIP. I let it go for a while, but it kept happening, so I inquired again. One of my girls told me that Thompson wasn't thrilled she'd shown up. That he wasn't expecting her and sent her away. However, Bradly was there, parked in his vehicle, and he marched her right back, telling Thompson this was his gift. She stayed for two hours, but they did nothing but play cards."

"That's weird. Where was that?"

"A motel in DC," Haven said.

"Thompson is a second lieutenant in the Army. He's also worked a few JSOC missions." Weston tapped his fingers on another stack of papers. "And Gorgen is FBI. He has a reputation for being as straight as they come." Weston shuffled through a few other sheets of paper. "He's known as an under-cover agent. He's been given medals for his work. I'm shocked that his name would be in this book."

"Do you know him?"

Weston shook his head. "The only thing I know about him is what I've read in a few reports that relate back to my case. I need to call Fenmore, but before I do that, tell me what you know about him."

"Nothing. Unlike Wicker, I never met him or Thompson."

"Okay, how did you meet Wicker?"

"He came to the house a few times to have meetings with Bradly. It wasn't often and usually late at night. The conversations were often heated. I could hear their raised voices, but I could never hear what they were saying. I figured Wicker wasn't satisfied with the girl because the names always changed whereas Thompson always got the same girl." She found the book pages and showed Weston the Thompson entries. "He had Helena five times. Gorgen only has two entries."

"Both men are married, not that it makes a difference." Weston rubbed his scruffy face. His beard had thickened since his arrival. She found it incredibly sexy. It gave him an edgy look, something that normally didn't intrigue her, but on Weston, it gave a cool, relaxed exterior, instead of the brooding attitude he'd arrived with. "Thompson has a bit of a sketchy military record. He's been passed over for a few promotions due to his inability to follow orders. But that doesn't necessarily mean anything. I'm sure my record doesn't read all that great either. But if both Thompson and Gorgen worked with Wicker on a JSOC, then we might have a connection."

"What does this have to do with getting Bradly out of my life?" She waved her hand over the table.

"This all seems so complicated. All I want is for him to leave me alone."

"He's never going to do that until he's behind bars. The bigger the crime, the longer we can put him away." He took her hands. "The escort agency is only one part of this. A smaller piece of the puzzle. I think he's using it to blackmail some of these officials to get what he needs for whatever illegal activities he's doing. Possibly drug running. Or bringing guns in or out of the country. We get him on all those things, he goes away for life. He'll never have the chance to hurt you or anyone else again."

A deep, hungry, guttural sob filled her throat. It was a mix of hope and anger. She desperately wanted Bradly to pay for his crimes. She didn't care what form that took. But she resented her sudden frustration over Weston's potential motivation. The connection between Wicker and Weston's case was undeniable. She tugged her hands away.

"Babe, what's wrong?"

"Are you doing this for me? Or for yourself?" She reached across the table and snagged her wine. It burned as it hit her already sour belly. It shouldn't bother her even if that were the case. He had a right to have his dishonorable discharge overturned. She understood the stigma that came with the branding.

It would forever be a dark cloud that followed him wherever he went. He wouldn't be able to follow his dream in law enforcement without having it changed. Who was she to judge him for wanting to have it removed?

He held her gaze, tugging her chair closer. The kindness seeping from his sweet eyes coated her skin like the sun. "All of this is for you."

"But the connection to Wicker and what it could mean—"

He pressed his finger over her lips. "While having Wicker arrested would help my case, it's not a slam dunk in overturning my discharge. It will only serve to show he's not a credible witness to what happened on the ground. It won't prove that the intel he received was false and that's what I need. But first things first. Our priority is Bradly and making sure you're safe. We'll deal with me and my problems after that."

"I'm sorry. I don't mean to question your motives in helping me. I already struggle with Zeke and your cousins."

"They're good people and part of it has to do with the way we were raised and the careers we had." He tucked a few stray strands of wet hair behind her ears. "I also like you, so my motives could be tainted by the notion that I want him gone so we can explore what this is without that hanging over our heads."

Heat flowed through her veins, landing on her cheeks. "I shouldn't trust sweet talk like that."

"Only, it's not sweet talk. The last thing I want to do is manipulate you into anything. I only want to be honest. Although, sometimes a good compliment goes a long way." He ran his thumb over her lower lip. "This might sound strange, but I'd do this whether or not I had feelings for you. The only difference is the urgency that I feel in my heart." He placed the palm of her hand in the center of his chest. "I would do it not because my cousins asked me, though that's part of it, but because I hate bullies. I can't sit back and do nothing when men like Bradly and Wicker are hurting people. It's why I've let Fenmore open my case. Otherwise, I would have walked away and forgotten all about it."

"But you let Ted and Darlene get away with their bullshit."

"The only person they hurt was me, and maybe themselves. They moved away because anyone who cared to know the truth, got it. But the difference there is an innocent child was involved. I wasn't going to do anything that might damage that little girl."

Haven palmed his cheek while she gazed into his beautiful, loving eyes. Weston was everything she could have ever dreamed of. She could absolutely describe him as the perfect man.

Her own Prince Charming.

"I can't help but be mad at Rocky and Ethan for the way they treated you for the last ten years."

"You're sweet, but I deserved some of it. It took the Darlene situation to turn me around." He leaned in and kissed her tenderly. It was soft and warm, and it sizzled across her skin, reminding her that she was a woman with wants. Desires.

Needs.

And they hadn't been met in years. If ever.

Straddling him, she tugged at his shirt, desperate to feel his hot skin pressed against her body. Her breath came in short pants. She tossed his shirt across the room and lifted hers over her head in record time. There was no fear. No insecurity. She wanted him in ways that she didn't understand. She didn't question it. Everything about him felt right. Normal. As if this was how it was supposed to be. She pressed her mouth over his, commanding his tongue in a wild dance.

"Hey," he whispered, lifting her chin. "Babe, slow down." Gently, he kissed her neck. His hands slid around her waist, cupping her ass. He sucked on her earlobe.

She gasped, arching her back. Her lungs burned. Fear crawled across her skin, starting at her toes, climbing up her calves, and swirling in her belly. Was he telling her to ease up because he didn't want her? She swallowed. Hard. An unwanted tear escaped from the corner of her eye.

He kissed it away. "Why are you crying?" He cupped her face, holding it steady, staring into her eyes with an exploring gaze that sucked the breath from her airways. "Did I do something wrong? Did I hurt you?"

"Um. I… why do you… um… want to slow down?" she managed to sputter. She sounded like a pathetic, insecure loser. This was not the young woman who'd ventured off to college at twenty-one. Bradly had stripped her of her dignity and her sexuality. She waffled between her desire to express her deepest emotions with Weston to needing to hide behind her biggest fears. She pressed her hands against his shoulders and pushed, turning her head.

"Oh no, you don't." He lifted her from his lap, setting her ass on the table, his fingers firmly gripping her waist. "You're not going to ask me a question and then run." He lifted her chin. "To answer you, I want to savor being with you, but we're also sitting at the kitchen table. I prefer a bed, to be honest. I also want to take things slow. I haven't had a real relationship in years and I'm in way over my head. I have no idea what I'm doing and I don't want to screw things up." Lifting her legs, he wrapped them around his waist before pressing his lips gently over her mouth. "I never thought I'd want to be with someone in any real, meaningful way again. I can't stop thinking about what it would be like to wake up with you in my arms every day, but that scares the shit out of me. I've fucked up every good thing that has ever come my way."

For the first time since Bradly had destroyed her life, she believed she held the power to change her world. To sit in the captain's seat and pilot her way to whatever destination she chose. Weston's insecurities weaved through her system like a small vessel lost on a dark, stormy night in search of safe passage.

It dawned on her that she was his lighthouse as much as he was hers. They were two broken souls navigating, leaving behind a cruel past, finding their way to their safe harbor.

"I'm scared, Weston. I'm scared I'll never be rid of

Bradly. I'm afraid that my past—what I did, who I was—will somehow end up between us the second you wake up in the morning. But mostly I worry this isn't real. That what you're feeling isn't—"

"Do you care about me?"

"Very much."

"Is that real?"

She nodded.

"Then trust that it's reciprocated. We both need to get out of our heads and stop letting the past—the people who hurt us—affect what we mean to each other." He shook his head. "Jesus, I sound like one of those damn movies on that cheesy romance network."

"Yeah, you do." She kissed the center of his chest. "It's crazy how much I feel for you."

"No crazier than mine for you." He reached for his cell.

"What are you doing?"

"Checking to make sure we can relax and do nothing for the next hour."

"Anything important?" she asked.

"Two texts from Ethan. There's something he's working on, but no details. He just says it's promising and he'll be in touch soon." He lifted her off the table, carrying her through the kitchen, down the short hallway, and kicking open the bedroom door. Gently, he laid her on the bed, his weight between her legs. "We can snuggle, watch a movie, or…" He winked.

Gunner jumped on the bed, circling near their heads until he found his sweet spot.

"Sorry, dude. You're going to have to go somewhere else for a little bit." Weston gave her dog a good shove.

Gunner whimpered but didn't put up too much of a fight as he leaped off the bed, stopping at the door to glance over his shoulder before trotting off into the other room.

"I don't understand. I got that dog because he doesn't trust men, but all of a sudden he is loyal to you?" She rolled Weston to his back, straddling him while she removed her bra. She reveled in his deep guttural growl and appreciative wide eyes. The few men she'd been with besides Bradly looked at her with lust, but they didn't admire her or make her feel desired. No, they made her want to wash her body with scalding water and the strongest of soaps. Their touch lingered on her skin like a bad rash that wouldn't go away whereas Weston's touch stayed with her like a warm blanket that kept her safe.

"He has a good sense of who can be trusted and

knows I'd never do anything to hurt you." Weston lifted his head, kissing the underswell of her breast. "Only, the condoms I rolled into town with are in my apartment."

Her body froze and not just in movement. All the heat that had been exploding inside, turned into a winter storm. The reality of her actions hit her with the full force of a hurricane.

"Don't go there." Weston took her chin with his thumb and forefinger. He stared deep into her eyes with an intense, but loving glare.

"How would you know where my mind wandered?"

"Because I know you and you're thinking about the other reason people use condoms besides birth control. You're worried if I'm going to suddenly be upset over the things in your past, but let's remember, I have a checkered one too. I've been called a womanizer more times than I can count, and while it's not entirely true, it's not false either. And considering I'm ten years older, it's possible I've slept with more people than you have."

"You're not trying to forget their names." She sucked in a deep breath and let it out in one big swoosh.

He laughed. "Some I wouldn't mind, and there

are a few I'm not sure I knew their names to begin with." He traced a path with his finger from her chin to her belly button. "With you, I want to remember every single thing. No matter what happens down the road, I never want to forget a second of my time spent in your presence."

"You really are a dork and you need to work on your lines." She rolled her eyes. "I don't have any condoms. I never expected that I would need them, but I think we should be safe, even though I'm taking the pill. Bradly and I didn't have sex often and honestly, he didn't send me out all that much except when he was pissed. But who knows who he's been with."

Weston pushed himself to a sitting position, holding her on his lap. "Did you get tested?"

She nodded. "It was all negative, but I need to retest. Some of that stuff could take months to show up and I wouldn't want to risk it." God, she hated this. It wasn't normal to have these kinds of conversations with a boyfriend.

Boyfriend? Was that what Weston was? Or could be? Did she even want that? Yes. She desperately wanted to be in his arms. More than once. The normalcy of it all felt too right. As if their shared disruptive pasts made for a smooth path forward —together.

"I'll be right back." He kissed her nose.

"Where are you going?"

He stood at the edge of the bed with a crinkled nose. He jerked his thumb over his shoulder. "Condoms. My apartment."

"I haven't scared you off yet?"

He laughed. "Not in a million years. Now, why don't you get all sexy under the covers. I won't be more than a couple of minutes."

She scooted to the top of the bed, pulled back the covers, and pulled them over her legs. With the blood rushing through her veins, bringing heat to all the important parts of her body, she shimmied out of her jeans and underwear, tossing her tiny thong at Weston.

Holding it up with his index finger, his jaw slacked open. He cleared his throat. "I better hurry up."

CHAPTER ELEVEN

Weston raced between the two apartments, making a beeline for his dresser. He'd barely spent any time in his studio since blowing into town. He kept his clothes and stuff there because he didn't want Haven to feel like he'd moved in. He certainly wasn't going to bring a box of condoms over, even though he had hoped he'd need them one day.

There was a part of him that worried it was too soon. Or it wasn't the right time solely because Bradly was still in town. He patted his back pocket. His phone was still on the kitchen table. It had only been fifteen minutes since the last time he checked. It wasn't a lot of time, but that didn't mean something couldn't have happened. He should have brought both his and Haven's into the bedroom. No matter what they had planned, they needed to keep their cells close by.

Bradly was playing the long game. He was patient, and it had become obvious he was willing to wait to show his hand.

Weston found the package he'd come for and turned. "Fuck," he muttered as he stared at Bradly, who smiled, pointing a gun in Weston's face. He sighed. He'd royally screwed up. His cousins would kill him, if Bradly didn't do it first.

"We meet again," Bradly said.

"What the fuck are you doing here? I should call the cops. This is considered trespassing." Only, he had no way of doing that. But Bradly didn't know he didn't have his cell. However, Weston didn't know how many men and women had come with Bradly and if they were in Haven's apartment.

His heart dropped to the pit of his stomach. He cared about Haven more than any woman since his early twenties. Hell, he had more feelings for Haven than for Darlene and he'd believed he'd been in love with Darlene. But the more he thought about it, the more he realized Darlene had used him like a puppy in a window. He represented what Darlene believed her life should be, instead of what made her happy.

"It's dangerous to tell a man holding a weapon

that you'll sic the police on him. For all you know, I might get a little trigger-happy in the process." Bradly smacked his lips, making a clucking noise like a goddamned chicken.

"Discharging a gun in my direction wouldn't be smart."

"It wouldn't be stupid, either." Bradly smiled. "Aren't you going to ask how I ditched your friends?"

"All right. How'd you manage that?" One of two things was happening. Either someone else was entering Haven's apartment and this was a distraction. Or Bradly wasn't concerned about her at the moment.

Weston banked on the latter simply because of his arrogance. When it came to women in their lives, men like him preferred to do their own dirty work.

The longer Weston kept Bradly talking, the more likely Haven would look at her phone—or his—and learn that Bradly had gotten the slip. Weston needed to give Haven as much time as possible to get the hell out.

"Your friend Wicker helped." Bradly waggled both brows.

"What makes you think he and I are friends?" Weston needed to understand the relationship between Wicker and Bradly. That was the key to unlocking the mystery of the book. He also wondered if this had to do with whatever Ethan had been working on. Fuck, Weston shouldn't have left his phone on Haven's kitchen table.

"Perhaps *friend* isn't the correct word choice in this situation, but he wasn't surprised to learn you'd landed in this sleepy town when you were given the boot from the Army," Bradly said. "He's been quite the fountain of information when it comes to you and your cousins."

"Oh, I'm sure," Weston muttered. He could only imagine the lies Wicker had told Bradly. That could work to Weston's advantage in dealing with his current dilemma.

"Wicker's currently in a limo pretending to be me with Zelda, heading back from a dinner with the real estate developers. Wicker will do whatever it takes to ensure the demise of you and your cousins. You've really pissed him off."

"The feeling's mutual." Weston squared his shoulders. "What do you want?"

"You're going to collect Haven and the book, and we're going to go for a little drive."

"I'm not going to do that." Weston planted his hands on his hips. "She's not going anywhere with you. However, I'll get you the book and you and I can go wherever you want."

"This isn't a negotiation."

"Then we have a problem." Weston pursed his lips.

"Not really." Bradly narrowed his left eye and shifted his right arm, aiming the weapon at Weston's left shoulder.

Bang!

Weston's body jerked back. Searing pain registered in his brain. "You motherfucking asshole." He grabbed his shoulder. Blood trickled through his fingers. He glanced down. The bullet went in his body and out his back. He'd need pressure on both sides or in a few hours, he'd bleed to death. "That wasn't necessary."

"I beg to differ. Now, I want what's mine. That's the book and Haven. Either you cooperate or you die. It's that simple. I don't need you to get what I want. I'm taking you to Wicker as a favor to him; otherwise, you'd already be dead." Bradly grabbed Weston by his good arm and shoved him in the direction of the door. Bradly's cell rang. "Hang on. I need to take this." He shoved him back on the bed. "Sit tight."

Weston breathed slowly. In through his nose and

out through his mouth. This wasn't good. Once again, he'd fucked up. Too many mistakes that he couldn't take back, and now lives—including his own—were at stake. However, Bradly was making a few of his own.

Firing his weapon had been a big one. Everyone in the building would have heard the shot. That meant it could have been reported, bringing the cops. Response time in this town was generally slow, maybe fifteen minutes. But if Haven heard it and managed to get a hold of his cousins, it would be less.

Weston had to trust Ethan and Rocky were already on their way.

HAVEN SMILED. Her insides filled with butterflies. She hadn't been this happy since… she had no idea. The intense fear had all but left. Some lingered in the deep dark recesses of her mind, but she trusted Weston. He was genuine. Kind. Sweet. A tad bit goofy. And he'd helped her regain her confidence. No matter where her past had brought her, Weston gave her a future.

Gunner came barreling into the bedroom with

her cell locked in his jaw. He dropped the slobbered-on device on the bed before turning and racing out of the room.

"Gross," she mumbled as she wiped the device. Before she could unlock the screen, Gunner dropped Weston's under her nose.

He hopped on the bed, whining, dropping his face on her hip. Two seconds later, his ears perked. A deep growl filled the air as Gunner showed his teeth. He jumped on all fours and let out a fierce bark, but he didn't leave the bed.

Haven's hand trembled as she stared at the text on her phone. She shifted her gaze toward Weston's.

There was a similar text along with two missed calls.

"Gunner. Protect the front door." She pulled back the covers, finding her clothes. She dressed as quickly as possible while her heart hammered in her chest like a machine gun.

Her dog leaped off the bed. He wouldn't let anyone in, not even Zeke, without ripping their leg off. The only man who had gained that dog's trust had been Weston. Hopefully, that would continue, because she wasn't about to open the door for anyone else.

Standing by the bedroom door, she tapped the

screen on her cell. Instead of texting Ethan back, she decided calling him would be better.

"Hey, Haven. Is everything okay?" Ethan asked. "Did you get our texts? We tried calling, but no one answered."

"I think so." She rubbed her temple. "Weston went to his place for a second, but he didn't take his phone, so he hasn't seen your message. He doesn't know Bradly slipped out."

"Fuck. We sent that text over twenty minutes ago. What the hell have you two been… never mind."

"It's not like that. We weren't doing anything. Well, not that," she said. "And I don't owe you an explanation. Nor does Weston. We had been going through all the documentation and we were exhausted. I—"

"I get it," Ethan said. "You took a break. We're all human and my cousin isn't a bad guy. Actually, he's one of the good ones. If the two of you like each other, well, who am I or Rocky to get in the way of that. But we sent him a slightly different text than you and it's important he reads it."

"I'm looking at his phone now."

"You have access to it?" Ethan asked with a shocked tone.

"He gave me the code in case something ever

happened." She scanned the words. "The FBI has an undercover agent and that man is Gorgen? And he's here? Are you shitting me?"

"No. We met with him right before that text. He wants to set up a sting operation, but there's a catch. We don't like it, and Weston's going to—"

Bang!

Gunner went nuts.

Haven dropped to the ground. She crawled across the bedroom floor. "Gunner. Come." She snapped her fingers. But the damn dog sat at the front door, growling and barking like it was the end of the world.

"Was that a gunshot?" Ethan asked.

"Yes," she whispered.

"Rocky, call 9-1-1. Get them to Haven's," Ethan said. "Haven. You listen to me very carefully. Put your phone in an inconspicuous place but leave it on. Take Weston's phone. Make sure the location services are turned on. Delete all the text strings from me, Rocky, and Zeke. When you can, inform Weston of what's happening, but only when it's safe. We don't want to blow Gorgen's cover. Whatever Bradly wants, for now, do it. We'll find you."

"What if he killed Weston?" Tears poured from her eyes.

"Bradly's not stupid and doing that before he gets what he wants would be about the dumbest thing he could do. He can't afford to kill an ex-Ranger and leave him in his apartment. Bradly has a plan and I bet it includes making Weston look like either he shot you or you shot him. Or a million other things. But just do as I say. We're already on our way. We'll be following and we'll be in touch. Now hide that phone and leave it on. Do it now."

"Okay." She stood in the middle of the bedroom, wondering where to best set the phone.

The nightstand.

Weston's gun.

Quickly, she raced to the side of the bed he'd claimed. He'd been so kind and considerate of her feelings and she cherished every moment she'd spent in his arms. She pulled open the drawer and pulled out his weapon. She wasn't the best shot, but she could hit a stop sign from twenty-five feet away. That wasn't nothing. She tucked it into her over-sized sweatpants and pulled her sweater down.

She brought the cell out into the family room and set it on the coffee table between a couple of maga-zines. She thought that might be the best place for it. She checked her phone, deleting the texts and double-checking the location settings.

"Haven," Weston called. "Put a leash on Gunner."

"Are you okay? I thought I heard something that sounded like a gunshot. But maybe it was a car back-firing?" There was no way Weston would have her leash Gunner over anything other than someone coming to the door with him who Gunner might not appreciate. She snagged Gunner's leash and hooked it to his collar.

The dog did not like being pulled away from the door. His nails scraped on the floor and his growl didn't ease up.

"Make sure Gunner's tethered to something." The front door inched open.

"Weston? What's going on?" She tied Gunner to the kitchen island.

He stumbled through the door, gripping his bare shoulder. Blood oozed through his fingers down his chest and across his stomach. "It's nothing." He held her gaze, his face as white as a ghost. His eyes were gray and cloudy.

Without thinking, she turned, snagging a towel. She pressed it against the open wound. She gasped when Bradly stepped into her space. Her home. It would forever be tainted now.

Gunner snarled and lunged forward. The leash snapped him back and he whimpered.

"Sit, Gunner," Weston commanded. "Now."

Gunner growled and then whined. He sat at Weston's feet, staring up at him with utter sadness etched in his eyes. But his hair stood on end and it was as if he were waiting for Weston to give him the okay to attack.

"Why the fuck did you shoot him, Bradly? He has nothing to do with this." The cold metal of Weston's gun pressed hard against her skin as it wedged between her underwear and her body. "You could have killed him."

"It's a flesh wound," Bradly said with a laugh.

"I beg to differ." She held her hands firmly against both sides of Weston's shoulder.

"I've been in worse shape from a gunshot wound, trust me." He patted her hand. "We need to get the book. The original." Weston arched a brow.

She held his gaze. Her heart stuck her throat like a thick piece of doughy bread that wouldn't budge. "It's at the bar," she said a little louder than her normal voice. Maybe she could give Ethan, Rocky, and Zeke a head start. Surprise Bradly before they even got there.

Weston's eye twitched. His lips drew into a tight line.

Bradly laughed. "By the looks of it, your

boyfriend would have tried to stall by taking us somewhere else." He inched closer, but Gunner was on his feet in less than a second, showing his teeth. "Tell that dog to stand down or I'll put a bullet in his head."

"Gunner, knock it off," Weston said. "And no, I wouldn't have done that. I thought it was here." He tilted his head. "Why'd you move it without telling me? I thought you trusted me."

She shrugged. "It's nothing personal, but I barely know you."

Weston had been the one to put the original in the safe at On the Rocks. It had been his idea. All this chatter was smoke and mirrors to throw Bradly off. Only, Weston didn't know his cousins were listening. She needed to find a way to inform him of that little fact. Creativity wasn't one of her strong suits.

"One thing you don't know about my little girl is, she doesn't need to know someone to fuck them." Bradly held up a condom and smiled. "You haven't changed, which is good for me. You'll fall in line right quick when you come home."

"You can have the book, but you can't have me," she said with more conviction than she'd had in a long time. She was tired of being scared. Of looking over her shoulder, wondering when Bradly would show up and destroy what little life she had carved out for herself.

No more.

Bradly raised his weapon, pointing it at the center of Weston's chest.

She jumped in front of Weston, but he strong-armed her out of the way. She turned and glared. "I'm not going to stand here and let him kill you over a stupid book, or over me." She turned. "He knows nothing and isn't important. I'll give you the book, and then you and I are done. I'm not going to stand in your way. The last two months prove I'm no threat to you."

"Little girl, that's not the point, and whether or not I have a beef with him isn't the problem. I'm not going to stand here and argue with you." He waved his gun. "Now, let's go, or I will put a bullet in that man's heart."

Weston groaned as he stood. "It's best if we do as he says."

She sighed. As long as Bradly didn't search her, she still had an ace up her sleeve with the cell in her pocket and the gun in her underpants. "Fine. But I swear to God, Bradly. If you hurt any of my friends, I won't keep my mouth shut."

"I'd be careful about threatening me." Bradly pointed to the door.

Holding on to Weston, she inched toward the front of the apartment.

Gunner tried to follow, but the leash held him back. He didn't like that, and he let his frustration show as he continued to claw at the floor. His growl was low and deep. He yelped, jumping on his hind legs. He shifted his body, glancing between Weston and Haven, before turning his head toward the kitchen window.

Haven found that odd. They were on the fourth floor. There shouldn't be anything that caught his attention.

Except the fire escape.

A shadow eased across the opening.

She wasn't going anywhere. Not now. Not ever. Reaching into her sweats, she pulled out Weston's weapon. "On second thought, I'm not giving you anything." With a shaky hand, she raised the gun, pointing it at Bradly's chest. She held her breath.

Bradly's smile quickly turned to a frown.

"What the fuck," Weston whispered.

Gunner stopped growling and lay on the floor, putting his head on his paws. He only did this under two conditions. It was commanded or he felt safe.

There was nothing safe about this situation. Whoever was on the other side of that window had to have given Gunner the command. The only people who had that kind of rapport with Gunner were Brayden and Zeke. While Gunner didn't like men, he tolerated Brayden and Zeke. They had an understanding. Gunner could be around the rest of the crew but didn't have the same aggressiveness with Brayden and Zeke as he did with most men. It wasn't the same as with Weston, but Gunner would listen to them when she was around.

"Put that thing down." Bradly shifted his gun between Weston and Haven. "You shoot and one of you will end up dead. That's not the outcome you want. Besides, with how badly your hand is trembling, you'll miss me altogether."

"I don't think so." She focused on Bradly's chest.

"Haven," Weston whispered. "Give me the gun. This isn't the way to deal with this situation. He'll kill us without batting an eyelash. And I don't think you want to live with the aftermath of pulling that trigger."

"He's right," Bradly said. "Because it's not you I'm going to kill, it's him. Do you really want to watch someone you care about die? I mean, you almost lost your dad because you refused to come home."

"I knew that was you." Anger darkened her heart. "You're a fucking piece of shit. I'm not going to be terrorized by you anymore."

"Listen to me, Haven." Weston placed his hand on her biceps. "Right now is the time to cooperate."

"No," she said. "I'm done doing what that man wants me to do. Besides, I know a few things that neither one of you do." She jerked her chin toward Gunner.

Weston glanced to the floor. He arched a brow.

"What do you think you know, little girl?" Bradly asked with an amused smile.

"For starters, you have a big fat fucking leak in your organization." She gripped the gun tighter. She hadn't expected it to take this long for the gang to come charging through the door or window or even the goddamned wall. The longer she held the weapon, the heavier it got.

"Right. Tell me another one." Bradly shifted his stance.

"It's true. One of your VIP clients is an under-cover agent. He's been gathering intel on you for over a year," she said.

"Excuse me." Weston snapped his gaze back to her. "That's brand-new information."

"A lot happened while you were back at your

apartment," she said.

"I'm bored with your stalling tactics." Bradly inched closer.

Gunner lifted his head and growled, stopping Bradly in his tracks.

Bradly held his weapon steady, right at Weston. That was something that did worry Haven.

"Move or I'll kill him," Bradly said in a deep tone. "And give me that thing." He snatched the gun from her fingertips. Pressing his weapon in the center of her back, he shoved her toward the door. He did the same thing to Weston.

Two seconds later, the sound of guns clicking rang in her ears. Weston heaved her to his bloody chest, pushing her against the wall.

"Freeze, motherfucker," Zeke said, holding a large rifle pointed at Bradly.

Ethan and Rocky flanked his left and right, also with incredibly massive weapons.

Brayden stepped from the apartment just as Bradly tried to turn to make his way back inside. "You're not going anywhere." Brayden snagged Bradly's gun.

"Oh, yes, I am," Bradly said. "You goons aren't cops. You have no right to detain me. I was defending myself against these two. You have no idea what we've been through."

Zeke laughed, holding up a cell. "Actually, we know everything because we've been listening."

Ethan took a step forward. "And so have the FBI. You're fucking toast. You'll be going to jail for a very long time."

The sound of boots hitting the stairs filled her ears. Men wearing FBI jackets came flying up the steps.

"We'll take it from here," one of them said. "We thank you for your service."

"Anytime, man." Zeke nodded.

Ethan ripped off his shirt, pressing it against Weston's wounds. "We better get you to the hospital."

Haven raced to his side as he collapsed to the floor.

"I was really in the dark during that exchange," Weston said weakly. "I'm sorry. I fucked up royally again."

"Not really." Rocky patted his good shoulder. "But you do have a smart as fuck girlfriend. Although, I really wish she hadn't pulled out that gun. That could have gone sideways."

"But it did buy us some time," Zeke said.

Haven helped Ethan put pressure on the other side of the wound. "I was so scared, but when I saw Gunner lie down and the shadow in the window, I decided to turn the tables. It's the only thing Bradly understands." She glanced up, watching the federal agents put the cuffs on Bradly. He cussed them out, promising to have their jobs on a silver platter. They took him down the steps as the paramedics passed them.

"I'm sorry I put you in that position." Weston coughed. "I shouldn't have left you. This is all my fault."

"I'm the one who should be apologizing. He shot you because of me." She pressed her lips over his mouth.

"You two are pathetic," Ethan said. "Young love. It's disgusting sometimes."

"Excuse us, ma'am. We needed to check his vitals and get him to the hospital," the paramedic said.

"Can I ride with him?" she asked.

The paramedic nodded.

She glanced up at Zeke. "Thank you. For everything. I know this might not all be over—"

"We got him dead to rights," Zeke said. "He won't ever be able to hurt you or anyone you care about again."

The tears came hot and fast.

"Babe, don't cry," Weston said weakly. "I can't stand it when you do that." He took her hand and squeezed.

She sucked in a deep breath and swiped at her cheeks. She gazed into Weston's loving eyes. "I hope you heal quickly because we have unfinished business."

Weston smiled like a big kid. "I'm sure all I need is a few stitches, and I don't need both arms to—"

"Okay, we don't need to hear any more of this shit." Ethan laughed. "But you should know, he's a big baby. He broke his arm when he was ten and he cried for days. We all had to wait on him. It was just sad."

"I will gladly be his nurse." For the first time in years, Haven believed she had a future.

CHAPTER TWELVE

Weston shifted, groaning. The painkillers had fried his brain. He couldn't believe that he had needed surgery to repair the damage from the bullet. Worse, that he was going to need to spend the next twenty-four hours in the hospital and not in Haven's bed. All he wanted to do was hold her with his good arm, kiss her, and tell her how much he cared. Nothing else mattered. Not even his dishonorable discharge.

A tap at the door startled him, making him jerk, sending another searing jolt through his shoulder.

"Hey, man, how you holding up?" Ethan strolled through the entrance to his room.

"I'll be better when they let me out of this joint."

"The doctor said the surgery went well and that there was no significant damage."

"I should be good as new in six weeks," Weston said. "Maybe sooner. I can start physical therapy in a couple of days."

"I'm glad to hear that." Ethan smiled. "I have some good news for you."

"What's that?"

"I just got off the phone with Fenmore."

Weston did his best to sit more upright, but it was hard with only one good arm. "She called you?" He reached for his cell. He'd been checking it every ten minutes since he'd woken up from surgery. Not because he wanted to hear from Fenmore, but because he wanted Haven. He was disappointed that she hadn't been by his side and was the first thing he saw when he blinked open his eyes. The nurse informed him that she was with her father and he understood. He wasn't angry or anything, especially since her dad had woken up and had been able to confirm that it had indeed been Bradly who had hit him with his vehicle.

Another nail in that coffin.

"There were some loose ends she needed from us regarding Bradly, but that also tied into Wicker and your case." Ethan sat on the edge of the bed. "I asked her if I could be the one to tell you." He held his facial expressions tight, giving nothing away.

"I'm all ears."

"The bad news is you won't be getting a new hearing."

Weston's heart dropped to his gut. He wasn't sure what felt worse. His shoulder or the weight of the news. "Why not?"

"Because the committee decided—based on the charges filed against Wicker and the fact he's rolling over on Bradly in order to try to save his own ass—that no hearing is needed to overturn your discharge." Ethan smiled. "Once the paperwork is filed and stamped, your discharge will be changed to an honorable discharge. Fenmore believes that will happen by the end of the month."

Weston's jaw dropped open. "Please don't fuck with me."

"I'm not. It's a done deal. You will be able to do whatever you want, including law enforcement, if you choose. Although, Rocky and I don't want you to leave Fallport. We like having you around."

"I like it here too."

Ethan laughed. "You like Haven."

"I won't deny that and she's one of the reasons I will choose to stay, if she'll have me."

"Oh, we all know the feeling there is mutual. You're all she can talk about." Ethan glanced toward the door. "She feels terrible about you getting shot. As if it's her fault."

"That one is on me."

"Stop that. You didn't make a mistake. And before you go into all the reasons why you think you did, no one blames you for what happened. Bradly was looking for a weak spot. He could have come at her from any front. Had you not been where you were, he probably would have gotten to her eventually. We couldn't have protected her the way you did."

"Who are you and what did you do with my grumpy-ass cousin?"

Ethan squeezed his forearm. "I'm sorry I doubted you for so long and there are a couple of other people on the other side of that door who want a fresh start too."

Weston blinked. "Who?"

"Your parents."

"They're here? How?"

"They just landed a little while ago. Can they come in?"

Weston nodded. The monitor that checked his heart rate beeped wildly. He wished he could turn it off. He didn't want his parents to know he was scared. He'd disappointed them so many times. He didn't want this to be another one.

Ethan pushed open the door and disappeared. Seconds later his mom inched into the room, followed by his father.

"Hello, son," his dad said. "It's been a hot minute."

His mom raced to his side, sitting on the edge of the bed and taking his hand. "I'm so sorry you got shot, but Haven told us what a hero you are and wow, what a sweet girl she is. Poor child has been through so much."

He narrowed his eyes. "What do you know about Haven?"

"Rocky filled us in on everything," his dad said. "And I mean, everything." He stuffed his hands in his pockets. "We should have known you'd never walk away from your own child. Or that Darlene would keep us from our grandchild. We have been terrible parents."

"I haven't been a model son."

"We've all made mistakes, but we'd like a second chance." His mom leaned in and kissed his forehead like she used to do when he'd been a small child. It was warm and loving, a sensation he'd missed most of his adult life.

"So would I," he managed to choke out. "So, you met Haven?"

"She's in the hallway," his dad said. "She thought

it would be good for us to spend a little time alone together. She's a kind girl. It's terrible what that man did to her. To her parents. We're glad he'll be going away for a long time."

"You and me both, because if he ever got out, that temper of mine wouldn't be contained." Weston wiped away the tear that had escaped his eye.

"We'd like to stay in Fallport for a few weeks, if that's okay with you." His father pulled up a chair.

"I live in a studio apartment, so I'd have to get you a hotel room."

"Haven said we could actually stay in your apartment since she's going to be nursing you back to health," his mom said with a beaming child. "I know I have no business giving you advice after all these years, but don't screw this up. She's a keeper."

Weston took his mother's hand and kissed it. "I think I'm falling in love with her."

"Well, fall faster, because that young woman is madly in love with you."

"ARE YOU COMFORTABLE?" Haven stuffed another pillow behind Weston's head.

Gunner did a dance at the foot of the bed, frustrated that he wasn't allowed on it.

"I'm perfect. Now why don't you stop fussing over me and climb in." Weston tugged at her arm.

"I should check on your folks."

"They're fine." He cocked his head. "Are you avoiding me?"

"No." She pulled back the covers and settled in next to the man she knew without a doubt that she loved. It should be a strange feeling, yet it felt perfectly normal. "I just want to make sure they have everything they need."

"It's midnight. They are sound asleep by now."

She wrapped her arm around Weston, resting her head on his chest, careful to stay away from his wound. "Are you in any pain?"

"Nope." He tilted her chin with this thumb and forefinger. "I was thinking I'd apply to the local police department."

"Really? What about the FBI?"

"I want to be here with you and being a cop is the next best thing to an agent."

"What if I still want to go that route?"

"Then I'll support you and we'll figure it out." He kissed her lips, soft and sweet.

"You act like we'll be together forever."

"I hope so." He ran his thumb over her cheek. "This might be crazy and perhaps way too soon, but I love you."

"We haven't even had sex yet. What if you hate making love to me?"

"Impossible, but why don't we find out right now." He jerked his head back. "Of course, my ego is fragile, and it would help to know if you had similar feelings."

"I do love you," she whispered. "But maybe we should wait until your body has had a chance to heal before we—"

"I can wait if you need more time, but it's not necessary. However, we'll need to do this a certain way."

Butterflies filled her stomach. They floated and fluttered through her system. Sex wasn't something she ever looked forward to, but with Weston, it wasn't only something she desired. It was what she knew love was supposed to be like. She eased out of her pajamas and helped him remove his boxers.

There was no shame in her actions or her nakedness. The heat that rose to her cheeks wasn't from embarrassment.

His kisses were filled with tender passion. He

touched her in ways she'd only ever imagined. Being with him was effortless. Making love to him was beyond her wildest expectation. She belonged in his arms, where she knew she would stay for the rest of her life.

EPILOGUE

Weston stood in the back of the auditorium, proudly wearing the Fallport Police Department uniform. He fiddled with his wedding ring. He and Haven were nearing their one-year anniversary and he was more in love with her today than he'd ever been. She was his sunshine in the morning. The water he drank. He couldn't imagine what his life would be like without her in it.

"It is with great pleasure that I present to you the newest officers of the Fallport Police Department," his captain said.

Weston puffed out his chest as *his wife* strode across the room wearing the same uniform. She'd done it. She'd made her dreams come true. Part of him worried she'd settled for being a police officer and not an FBI agent, but who was he to argue with her logic. They'd made a wonderful life for themselves in Fallport.

She'd mended fences with her parents. While there were still a few snickers here and there from ignorant people, most of the citizens of Fallport respected them both. Haven didn't want to leave the town in which she'd grown up in and she wanted to raise a family there.

When the time was right.

As each new officer shook the captain's hand, the crowd applauded.

Ethan slapped his back. "She's come a long way."

"Yes, she has," Weston admitted.

"Look at our little girl," Zeke said.

"I feel like a proud papa," Rocky added.

Weston laughed. He waved as Haven made a beeline for the group. He opened his arms and lifted her off the ground. "You did it, babe."

"I sure did, but the first year is going to suck since I'll be on desk duty," she said.

"Excuse me?" Weston set her feet on the ground and held her by the hips. "Why on earth would our captain do that? You're perfectly capable of being on patrol. That doesn't make any sense."

She took his hand and placed it over her stomach. "Well, Daddy. I think it's the right call, considering I'll be showing in about a month, and then I don't think it would be smart to be pregnant and out there on the streets."

Ethan, Rocky, and Zeke all burst out laughing.

Weston blinked. "Huh?" The words registered in his brain, but he hadn't fully processed their meaning. "Daddy? Baby? Pregnant?"

"You can repeat and question them all you want," Ethan said. "But that doesn't change the fact that you're going to be a father."

"I need to sit down." Weston stumbled to a chair. He ran a hand over the top of his freshly cut hair.

"Are you okay?" Haven asked, sitting on his lap. "I know we said we'd try next year, but this is what happens when we play Russian roulette with birth control."

He tucked a piece of hair that had fallen from her ponytail behind her ear. "Just in shock. I did not expect that. And I should be asking if you're okay."

"Are you happy about this?"

He smiled. "Babe, I'm thrilled. I really am. You know I've wanted to start a family. Again, this was unexpected. Are you sure?" He pressed his finger over her lips. "I'm only asking because I don't want either of us to be disappointed."

"I'm positive, Daddy."

"You're going to have fun calling me that, aren't you, Mommy?"

"Oh, I like that sound of that." She pressed her soft lips over his mouth. Haven had been what he'd been searching for his entire life.

Thank you for taking the time to read *Searching for Haven.* Please feel free to leave an honest review. If you'd like to know more about Darius Ford, Fenmore Harley, and Walther Mathis, please check out **Darius' Promise**.

ABOUT THE AUTHOR

Jen Talty is the *USA Today* Bestselling Author of Contemporary Romance, Romantic Suspense, and Paranormal Romance. In the fall of 2020, her short story was selected and featured in a 1001 Dark Nights Anthology.

Regardless of the genre, her goal is to take you on a ride that will leave you floating under the sun with warmth in your heart. She writes stories about broken heroes and heroines who aren't necessarily looking for romance, but in the end, they find the kind of love books are written about :).

She first started writing while carting her kids to one hockey rink after the other, averaging 170 games per year between 3 kids in 2 countries and 5 states. Her first book, IN TWO WEEKS was originally published in 2007. In 2010 she helped form a publishing company (Cool Gus Publishing) with *NY*

Times Bestselling Author Bob Mayer where she ran the technical side of the business through 2016.

Jen is currently enjoying the next phase of her life… the empty nester! She and her husband reside in Jupiter, Florida.

Grab a glass of vino, kick back, relax, and let the romance roll in…

Sign up for my Newsletter (https://dl.bookfunnel. com/82gm8b9k4y) where I often give away free books before publication.

Join my private Facebook group (https://www.facebook. com/groups/191706547909047/) where I post exclusive excerpts and discuss all things murder and love!

Never miss a new release. Follow me on Amazon:amazon.com/author/jentalty

And on Bookbub: bookbub.com/authors/jen-talty

NY STATE TROOPER SERIES (also set in the Adirondacks!)

In Two Weeks

Dark Water

Deadly Secrets

Murder in Paradise Bay

To Protect His own

Deadly Seduction

When A Stranger Calls

His Deadly Past

The Corkscrew Killer

Brand New Novella for the First Responders series

A spin-off from the NY State Troopers series

PLAYING WITH FIRE

PRIVATE CONVERSATION

THE RIGHT GROOM

AFTER THE FIRE

CAUGHT IN THE FLAMES

CHASING THE FIRE

Legacy Series

Dark Legacy

Legacy of Lies

Secret Legacy

Emerald City

INVESTIGATE AWAY

SAIL AWAY

FLY AWAY

Flirt Away

Colorado Brotherhood Protectors

Fighting For Esme

Defending Raven

Fay's Six

Darius' Promise

Yellowstone Brotherhood Protectors

Guarding Payton

Candlewood Falls

RIVERS EDGE

THE BURIED SECRET

ITS IN HIS KISS

LIPS OF AN ANGEL

Kisses Sweeter than Wine

It's all in the Whiskey

JOHNNIE WALKER

GEORGIA MOON

JACK DANIELS

JIM BEAM

WHISKEY SOUR

WHISKEY COBBLER

WHISKEY SMASH

IRISH WHISKEY

The Monroes

COLOR ME YOURS

COLOR ME SMART

COLOR ME FREE

COLOR ME LUCKY

COLOR ME ICE

COLOR ME HOME

Search and Rescue

PROTECTING AINSLEY

PROTECTING CLOVER

PROTECTING OLYMPIA

PROTECTING FREEDOM

<u>PROTECTING PRINCESS</u>

<u>PROTECTING MARLOWE</u>

DELTA FORCE-NEXT GENERATION

<u>SHIELDING JOLENE</u>

<u>SHIELDING AALYIAH</u>

<u>SHIELDING LAINE</u>

<u>SHIELDING TALULLAH</u>

<u>SHIELDING MARIBEL</u>

<u>SHIELDING DAISY</u>

The Men of Thief Lake

<u>REKINDLED</u>

<u>DESTINY'S DREAM</u>

Federal Investigators

<u>JANE DOE'S RETURN</u>

<u>THE BUTTERFLY MURDERS</u>

THE AEGIS NETWORK

The Sarich Brother

<u>THE LIGHTHOUSE</u>

<u>HER LAST HOPE</u>

<u>THE LAST FLIGHT</u>

ROUGH AROUND THE EDGES

ROUGH RIDE

ROUGH EDGE

ROUGH BEAUTY

The Brotherhood Protectors

The Saving Series

SAVING LOVE

SAVING MAGNOLIA

SAVING LEATHER

Hearts under Siege

Cove's Blind Date Blows Up

My Everyday Hero – Ledger

Tempting Tavor

Malachi's Mystic Assignment

Needing Neor

Holiday Romances

A CHRISTMAS GETAWAY

ALASKAN CHRISTMAS

WHISPERS

CHRISTMAS IN THE SAND

Heroes & Heroines on the Field

TAKING A RISK

TEE TIME

A New Dawn

THE BLIND DATE

SPRING FLING

SUMMERS GONE

WINTER WEDDING

THE AWAKENING

The Collective Order

THE LOST SISTER

THE LOST SOLDIER

THE LOST SOUL

THE LOST CONNECTION

THE NEW ORDER

There are many more books in this fan fiction world than listed here, for an up-to-date list go to www.AcesPress.com

You can also visit our Amazon page at: http://www.amazon.com/author/operationalpha

Special Forces: Operation Alpha World
Christie Adams: Charity's Heart
Linzi Baxter: Dangerous Rescue
Misha Blake: Flash
Anna Blakely: Rescuing Gracelynn
Julia Bright: Saving Lorelei
Cara Carnes: Protecting Mari
Kendra Mei Chailyn: Beast
Melissa Kay Clarke: Rescuing Annabeth
Gia Cobie: Saved from Revenge
Samantha A. Cole: Handling Haven
KaLyn Cooper: Spring Unveiled
Jordan Dane: Redemption for Avery
Tarina Deaton: Found in the Lost
D.M. Earl: Claire's Guardian
Riley Edwards: Protecting Olivia
Dorothy Ewels: Knight's Queen
Lila Ferrari: Protecting Joy
Nicole Flockton: Protecting Maria

Hope Ford: Rescuing Karina

Amy Gamet: Guarded by the SEAL

Desiree Holt: Protecting Maddie

Danielle Haas: Crossroads of Betrayal

Jesse Jacobson: Protecting Honor

Rayne Lewis: Justice for Mary

Ireland Lorelei: The Detective

Kristin Lynn: Worth the Risk

Callie Love & Ann Omasta: Hawaii Hottie

JM Madden: Rescuing Olivia

A.M. Mahler: Griffin

Ellie Masters: Sybil's Protector

Trish McCallan: Hero Under Fire

Naomi McKay: Twist

Rachel McNeely: The SEAL's Surprise Baby

KD Michaels: Saving Laura

Olivia Michaels: Protecting Harper

Annie Miller: Securing Willow

MJ Nightingale: Protecting Beauty

C.K. O'Connor: Delaney's Bodyguard

Melinda Owens: Betraying Katie

Victoria Paige: Reclaiming Izabel

Danielle Pays: Defending Sarina

Taryn Rivers: Savage Cove

Lainey Reese: Protecting New York

KeKe Renée: Protecting Bria

Taryn Rivers: Savage Cove

TL Reeve and Michele Ryan: Extracting Mateo

Ariana Rose: Chasing Paige

Deanna L. Rowley: Saving Veronica

Angela Rush: Charlotte

Rose Smith: Saving Satin

Tyler Anne Snell: Cowboy Heat

Lynne St. James: SEAL's Spitfire

E.M. Shue: Discovering Tyler

Bella Stone: Rexar

Jen Talty: Burning Desire

Reina Torres, Rescuing Hi'ilani

LJ Vickery: Circus Comes to Town

R. C. Wynne: Shadows Renewed

Delta Team Three Series

Lori Ryan: Nori's Delta

Becca Jameson: Destiny's Delta

Lynne St James, Gwen's Delta

Elle James: Ivy's Delta

Riley Edwards: Hope's Delta

Police and Fire: Operation Alpha World

Freya Barker: Burning for Autumn

B.P. Beth: Scott

Jane Blythe: Salvaging Marigold

Julia Bright, Justice for Amber
Gia Cobie: Saved from Revenge
Hadley Finn: Exton
Emily Gray: Shelter for Allegra
Danielle M. Haas: Crossroads of Betrayal
Deanndra Hall: Shelter for Sharla
Jenna Harte: Dead But Not Forgotten
Amber Kuhlman: Protecting Paisley
Reina Torres: Justice for Sloane
Aubree Valentine, Justice for Danielle
Maddie Wade: Finding English

Tarpley VFD Series

Silver James, Fighting for Elena
Deanndra Hall, Fighting for Carly
Haven Rose, Fighting for Calliope
MJ Nightingale, Fighting for Jemma
TL Reeve, Fighting for Brittney
Nicole Flockton, Fighting for Nadia

As you know, this book included at least one character from Susan Stoker's books. To check out more, see below.

<u>SEAL Team Hawaii Series</u>

Finding Elodie
Finding Lexie
Finding Kenna
Finding Monica
Finding Carly
Finding Ashlyn
Finding Jodelle

<u>Eagle Point Search & Rescue</u>

Searching for Lilly
Searching for Elsie
Searching for Bristol
Searching for Caryn
Searching for Finley
Searching for Heather (Jan 2024)
Searching for Khloe (May 2024)

<u>The Refuge Series</u>

Deserving Alaska
Deserving Henley

Deserving Reese
Deserving Cora
Deserving Lara (Feb 2024)
Deserving Maisy (Oct 2024)
Deserving Ryleigh (TBA)

SEAL of Protection: Alliance Series
Protecting Remi (July 2024)
Protecting Wren (Nov 2024)
Protecting Josie (TBA)
Protecting Maggie (TBA)
Protecting Addison (TBA)
Protecting Kelli (TBA)
Protecting Bree (TBA)

Delta Team Two Series
Shielding Gillian
Shielding Kinley
Shielding Aspen
Shielding Jayme (novella)
Shielding Riley
Shielding Devyn
Shielding Ember
Shielding Sierra

SEAL of Protection: Legacy Series

Securing Caite (FREE!)
Securing Brenae (novella)
Securing Sidney
Securing Piper
Securing Zoey
Securing Avery
Securing Kalee
Securing Jane

Delta Force Heroes Series
Rescuing Rayne (FREE!)
Rescuing Aimee (novella)
Rescuing Emily
Rescuing Harley
Marrying Emily (novella)
Rescuing Kassie
Rescuing Bryn
Rescuing Casey
Rescuing Sadie (novella)
Rescuing Wendy
Rescuing Mary
Rescuing Macie (novella)
Rescuing Annie

Badge of Honor: Texas Heroes Series
Justice for Mackenzie (FREE!)

Justice for Mickie
Justice for Corrie
Justice for Laine (novella)
Shelter for Elizabeth
Justice for Boone
Shelter for Adeline
Shelter for Sophie
Justice for Erin
Justice for Milena
Shelter for Blythe
Justice for Hope
Shelter for Quinn
Shelter for Koren
Shelter for Penelope

SEAL of Protection Series

Protecting Caroline (FREE!)
Protecting Alabama
Protecting Fiona
Marrying Caroline (novella)
Protecting Summer
Protecting Cheyenne
Protecting Jessyka
Protecting Julie (novella)
Protecting Melody
Protecting the Future

Protecting Kiera (novella)
Protecting Alabama's Kids (novella)
Protecting Dakota

New York Times, USA Today and *Wall Street Journal* Bestselling Author Susan Stoker has a heart as big as the state of Tennessee where she lives, but this all American girl has also spent the last fourteen years living in Missouri, California, Colorado, Indiana, and Texas. She's married to a retired Army man who now gets to follow *her* around the country.

www.stokeraces.com
www.AcesPress.com
susan@stokeraces.com

Made in United States
Cleveland, OH
13 May 2025